THING

SENSUAL AND SEDUCTIVE SHORT STORIES

Edited by

Anisa Larkwood & Jasmine Luck

ANISA LARKWOOD

Publishing

Cover design by Claire A. Jones, with photographs used under license from Canva Pro (https://www.canva.com)

Library of Congress Control Number: 2025900229

First edition

ISBN: 979-8-218-59419-0

Editing by Anisa Larkwood
Editing by Jasmine Luck

This book was professionally typeset on Reedsy.
Find out more at reedsy.com

To our brown-eyed boy, who started it all.

CONTENTS

PREFACE

This book began as a wild idea shared between two friends who both love reading (and writing!) romance stories.

It bloomed into an energetic and lively group project when we invited some of our favorite writers to contribute, and only now has it reached its final form—a book held in a reader's hands, ready to be devoured or savored as you see fit.

Each of these stories is a labor of love, a gift from the writer to the reader, and comprises what we hope is the first of many anthologies to come.

We're honored that you've chosen to join us. Happy reading!

-*The Editors, Anisa Larkwood & Jasmine Luck*

* * *

Content Warning: This book is intended for adults only (ages 18+). It contains fictional stories about sex and intimate relationships, and includes scenes of implied or explicit sexual activity between con-senting adults. Stories may also contain expletives and vulgar language, adult themes, and other items not suitable for minors.

SWIFT WARMING, SLOW BURN

♥ by O.J. Adira

The *hellos* went unspoken for a week or two. Every morning, scanning the light rail car as I found a seat, I'd look for the man in gray—gray stocking hat, white N95 mask, gray and green flannel scarf, gray puffer jacket—a seeming obelisk of a figure. And more mornings than not, the sun would glint off his reflective aviators like a beacon atop that tower, drawing my eye to his polite nod.

I wondered just how much those aviators hid; how often he could tell I'd lost my place in my book and let my eyes wander, sometimes to the city as it sped by outside the window, every low industrial building with its own plume of condensation rising off into the bone-shattering cold of the Midwestern winter sky.

But sometimes, I'd chase that glint of sunlight inside the train car and find it bouncing off those silvery sunglasses.

Perhaps we locked eyes on more than one occasion. I couldn't tell.

And I couldn't say if I'd ever really seen him prior to the incident.

* * *

It had been one of those days where a scarf was necessary, when the air was so cold it could put your throat in a deep freeze.

The power in my apartment had blinked out and then back on during the night, leaving me without a morning alarm. So I'd woken to a late start and a cold snap that left a frozen glaze over everything, including the front steps to my building—that would be the first fall—and the slick platform at the light rail station—that would be the second.

The third fall came as I stepped into the morning train and was sent sprawling by a bolting teen, a boy who realized just in time that it was his stop. He ran through the closing door, catching me with his shoulder, and I was down on the ground for the third time that morning.

I didn't get up right away. Not because I was hurting; but because I was trying not to cry. Too much misfortune, not enough spoons.

Later, I would chalk it up to imagination, but at that moment I thought I smelled cinnamon and chili. What was not imaginary was a gray glove appearing in my periphery and a man's smooth baritone.

"Are you okay?"

I wasn't.

"I'll be fine. I just—"

There was an immediate freedom from effort. The moment I accepted his hand, I was brought to my feet with a strength that belied his calm and quiet voice.

Coming up face to face—or, rather, scarf to scarf—with him, I wasn't prepared for what I found there.

Instead of connecting with the eyes of someone kind enough to help a complete stranger, I saw a pair of silver sunglasses reflecting my own shaken and tired expression. This pathetic look at myself was almost enough to send me over the edge. I would have burst out crying, were it not for the shock of finding myself in the helping hands of a completely masked stranger.

I don't know exactly what it was about him, but the first impression I had was one of safety. Of protection. Of a knight in silver armor.

Well, gray armor, anyway.

I stammered a, "Thank... you..." and as the train rocked into motion, I immediately hugged and clung to him. It was involuntary, a product of stress and hurry, of too much falling down and getting back up in one hour; both a literal and figurative play for stability.

I couldn't have known just how steady he really was.

Shocked by my behavior, I let go. I worked my chin above my scarf and forgot to apologize, skipping straight to rationalization by blurting, "I just had a really bad morning."

The man in gray paused. He nodded, and slowly let go of my shoulders. Then he turned away and sat down, directing his attention out the windows, allowing me to sit and cringe in silence.

After that day, he was no longer a stranger. He was often already on the train when I got on, always in the third car from the end, his presence somehow hard to ignore.

I'd give him a short nod to let him know I was still thankful for his kindness, and he would nod politely back in acknowledgment that all was well between us. At some unknown moment, those nods turned from *thanks* and *welcome* to a daily greeting.

But without words it was hard to tell when. And without seeing his face, it was hard to tell how.

* * *

There came a day when the stadium downtown was hosting a match between the city's biggest rivals. The morning train was nearly full and he was the first person I saw as I entered the car, waiting for me and waving me over.

At first I wasn't sure who I was looking at—the heavy gray coat replaced by a lighter blue jacket—but the mask and glasses gave him away. Moving his pack to the floor, he opened up one of the only available seats and it seemed rude to refuse.

"Hi, thanks," I said to his aviators as I took the kindness offered.

"Good morning," he returned, a little hesitant, a little awkward, but with a voice no less steady, and just as spreadable as buttercream. "You doing okay?"

I realized he was referencing our first interaction, now so many days prior. "Yeah, no bruises. Thanks for checking in. You okay?"

He chuckled, "For now."

Enigmatic. What did that mean? The little laugh was genuine. For the first time I realized that there was surely a face under all that wrapping that could smile, but I had no reference as to what that smile would look like. "Male" was all I had.

"For now? Like this moment in time, or today, or this year?"

Another little chuckle and a glance toward the

gloved hands in his lap. "More or less all of it. But this moment is pretty good."

He must have registered my subtle shift in my seat and realized that he came off as flirtatious.

"Sorry. Haven't been having a lot of casual conversations lately. I didn't mean—"

"Why not?" I smiled. This was a good opportunity to redefine whatever this was, to scrape the awkward dance of apologies and forgiveness away and get right to knowing the bundle of gray—er, blue—and mirrored aviators that I'd been forming a non-verbal relationship with these past few weeks.

I nodded toward his N95. "Did COVID kick your ass, too? How much time did you have to quarantine?"

The blank stare must have been reaction time to my forwardness. To be honest, I'd surprised myself.

"*Ah*... no. I mean. Not me. It's my nephew..."

I immediately regretted my comment. "Oh, no. I'm sorry. I didn't mean to pry. You don't know me and you don't have to tell me—"

I've never made the best first impressions with people. When you're a librarian, people generally believe that you're quiet and stern, too serious. I'd often tried to subvert that expectation, to be warm and approachable, especially with kids. But outside the stacks was a different story; I was out of context, a cook out of her kitchen, the most awkward of guests in the larger hotel of the world.

Having delved too far, too fast, I thought I should go back to the apologies and niceties, but I stopped in my tracks when he reached up to remove his sunglasses.

His eyes were brown. Not just brown, they were the color of comfort, of melted chocolate or a childhood teddy bear—right on the brink of black with a flash of rich golden red like the coat of a chestnut foal or tumbled tiger's eye, deep and warm and inviting me to fall in, promising that I would be caught and cared for. Lines spread from their outer corners—he was smiling—a reassurance that my apologies were not needed.

"Sometimes I forget that when I'm wearing these, nobody can tell how serious I am—or am not. I feel like I spent so much time during the pandemic relearning how to read someone without their facial expressions that I started forgetting about my own. I must be coming off as really creepy."

Under any other friendly, bookish circumstance, I may have found myself waving it off or making a joke—maybe even a "Hey, Brown Eyes, good to finally get to see you."

But the smooth sweetness of his mahogany irises was unexpected, and while I wanted to say that *I'd* been the one feeling like a creeper, there was a momentary lapse in my ability to do just about

7

anything more complicated than breathing.

I was surprised that he wasn't... what? Older? Rougher? Scarred up or missing an eye? He was built broad and sturdy, so I had formed an image in my mind of a pasty, block-headed linebacker under all those wraps.

Taking off his sunglasses had also dragged one dark curl out from under his stocking cap, proving him to be many things I was happily wrong about.

I could tell by the glint in his eye that he watched this dawn on me, and also that he enjoyed it. Generous, he let it slide.

"You're a librarian," he said.

Confusion must have lingered on my face, because he poked a knuckle against the well-worn tote bag on my lap, its sassy bespectacled dragon shushing a patron and accidentally blowing sequined fire at the same time.

"'Less burn, more learn,' huh?" he read, extending the metaphorical talking stick to me, not hiding the fact that he wanted to get to know me better.

Thank goodness. Suddenly, in that moment, it was everything I wanted, too.

His name turned out to be Alex—a favorite of mine—and paired with the brown eyes, the sonorous voice, and the very real scent of cinnamon and chili, he already had me by the romance section. By the time I found out that he had (until recently) been a bona fide hero in Firefighters Without Borders, I didn't care what lay under that N95.

Wow.

My morning commute began to rock between the worlds of complete yearning and utter despair, believing there was no way that Alex could be both this amazing *and* interested in me. I started to compartmentalize the ride to work as my little fantasy time, the dreamy half hour where a very chivalrous firefighter only had eyes for me. It was a bittersweet couple of months.

I heard stories of blazing infernos and the grateful village elders he helped to save, all the disasters he had worked through and the aid he provided. I couldn't hide the fact that I felt inadequate, with my reciprocal tales of setting up Science Sundays for the kids in my library. I told Alex that in comparison, I felt really lazy.

"What are you talking about?" he countered. "I just kept houses from burning. You actually nurture the minds of the next generation."

"But you saved *lives*," I said.

His eyes squinted above the mask and he rocked his shoulder into mine. He'd eschewed his blue jacket for a lighter green flannel as the days grew warmer, which meant less of a buffer between us.

"There's a good chance you do, too. You may have more influence than you know."

Is there such a thing as love-at-*no*-sight? That burst of emotion that catches you off guard when someone actually shows you how they see you, even if you can't see them?

I could feel my gaze drop to where his lips should be, an instinctual, human, heartfelt pull to connection... and then remembered there was a mask in the way. I might have died of embarrassment right then.

But I wasn't wearing a mask.

And he was getting the full advantage of that same instinct.

I managed to direct my attention out the window before our eyes could meet, to get a rein on my racing heart and pull it back under control before returning to the conversation as if I hadn't just nearly swooned all over him.

Not registering that he'd practically been doing the same.

* * *

It was around that time that I started dreaming about Alex. I'd dream that he came to find me at work, or that I'd bumped into him at the grocery store; nothing outlandish. But his face was never his face. It was Alex in the guise of some celebrity, or a boyfriend from my past. Sometimes he'd lean in to kiss me, but no matter how I yearned for it, I'd back away. Alex's eyes were there, warm and welcoming, but always in the wrong face, and I only wanted him—*his* eyes and *his* face—even though I couldn't know what the right face would be.

I would wake up and make sure to get to the platform on time, to get back to the real Alex. It slowly became apparent to me that I'd rather have him shrouded in mystery than have no trace of him at all.

* * *

One morning in early April, as the trees whipping by the train windows dripped with melting ice and I'd finally put my scarf and hat away for good, I asked him, "It sounds like you loved your job. So why'd you quit?"

By this time Alex was also going without a hat, his dark curls waving away from his face and pooling behind his ears with the mask loops. I could see his skin now—his olive complexion at his forehead and down his neck—and every new piece of him only made me more nervous about any future where I might see more.

I lived a life of books and he of fire; it felt like an attraction that could burn hot and fast, but could it ever be a good fit? As long as he was covered, he would always be perfect, but the longer I knew him, the more chance I had at being selfishly disappointed when he had less clothing to shield him.

But there are other ways for someone to reveal themselves to you.

The question sent his gaze dropping to his worn and rough hands, gloveless and folded in his lap, thumbs absently running over each other one after another.

"An accident. Car accident. My brother and his wife were killed."

"Oh my god, that's so sad. I'm so, *so* sorry."

"Yeah," his eyes took on a watery shine as he continued to watch his thumbs. "He was my only sibling, and our parents are gone. But his boy—my nephew, David—David survived the crash."

It was like someone had slammed the jaws of life into my heart and began to crack it open. "Oh my god. You're his only family."

"Yeah."

I didn't know where to go from there. Asking Alex what he did now to support himself and David seemed crass, and asking him about the child in his care felt invasive. I could only wait until he wanted to say more, but he had retreated in his head and his heart, neck bent and his shoulders stooped, and it was apparent that there was *so much* weighing him down. This man who told me of battling flames and climbing into trees, who carried grown men out of danger and barrels of water into it, was suddenly the one who needed a hand.

And so I put mine in his.

It's an interesting thing when you give support to someone who is used to being the hero. Someone who knows how to jump in and help another person in need, but who can't seem to make that jump to save themselves.

At first, Alex only stared at my hand in his, his folded prayer broken up, his thumbs finding still-ness. But a second later his warm fingers closed around mine, the other hand snapping around it, holding on, relying on me to keep him from falling in deeper. I was reminded of that first day when I had needed him, when I had held on for dear life.

Alex's voice was soft, but rough around the edges. "The kid's got leukemia, so he's been at the hospital downtown. I go down there every morning. Spend a few hours with him before work."

Ah. A child with a compromised immunity. Now the mask made more sense.

I looked at the LED clock at the front of the train car, half an hour before I had to open the library for the day. "They let you go in this early?"

He shook his head, the mask widening slightly to accommodate a small smile. "They won't accept visitors for another hour."

The way he swept his thumbs over my knuckles said, *Thank you for your kindness.*

The way he returned my hand reluctantly to my own lap said, *I don't want you to feel obligated.*

The way he bumped his shoulder against mine in the cheeky manner I'd become endeared to said, *It's worth it to go in an hour early because I get to ride this train with you.*

And the way I reached up to run my palm gently against his shoulder said, *I'm here for you.*

He closed his eyes with a sigh.

"Alex, my library's not far from the medical district. Come in, and let me make coffee for you?"

Another small smile crossed his face, crinkling the outer corners of those deep brown eyes and warming the space between us.

"Thanks," he said, his voice dipping low, trying to accept this generosity with grace—and humor. "Got any good books there?"

I snorted. "Just a few. What are you looking for?"

He thought a minute before looking up with an air of hope. "Cookbooks?"

"Sure, we have some. What kind of food?"

"I don't know yet. What's your favorite?"

Was he—?

"Oh... I don't know. I guess I like Indian?"

He chuckled. "Okay. Any particular region?"

I shrugged, "I like a good Bengalese?"

"I don't know that region. That means—?"

"Milder, smokier, sweeter. Starts off warm and builds to heat."

His flush was subtle, adding a little rose to his olive. "So, you like a slow burn? I could go for that."

"I guess so," I laughed. "I'm a bit of a weakling when it comes to heat."

"Good thing I know how to deal with fire." He paused, then drew in a breath and held it before using it to say, "You know, I get on the train just one stop before yours."

Oh my god, was he really—?

"Oh? That's a nice part of town."

He nodded. "It was my brother's house. He did alright for himself, but it's kind of empty. They're going to let David come home this weekend, and I'd really like to have a guest for dinner, but it's kind of hard to make friends in this town. Now I've got one I'd like to invite. You free Saturday?"

Oh, he was. He really was!

"I heard firefighters get to be real good cooks," I breathed.

"I think I can prove that rumor true," he said, standing as our stop was announced and the train neared the platform. "And I heard librarians are really good with kids. David will like you."

"We're fantastic with kids, actually." I took his

extended hand and joined him. "I think I'm free on Saturday."

"Great. Let's go find a recipe."

* * *

I'm not the type to get nervous before a first date. But I'll admit this time I was.

I needn't have worried.

Getting off the light rail on Saturday night, I could smell Alex before I saw him, the garlic and cumin and pepper crashing in a warm, welcome wave. The combination sent ripples of hunger through my gut, which gave an ample groan of want.

"Good, you came hungry."

I stopped still on the platform, looking toward the voice I'd come to know so well. I found a wavy, dark haired, brown-eyed man greeting the spring thaw in a deep burgundy flannel opened to a plain, clean white T-shirt that begged for an upward glance to a brilliant smile.

Alex's handsome, dimpled, *unmasked* smile.

Straight nose, sharp chin, high cheekbones.

I knew then that my days would be getting much more sunny and my dreams way more vivid. At least now, he'd always show up in them just right.

He stood with hands in jean pockets, grinning down at his feet until I met him toe to toe.

16

"Lots of garlic I'm getting off you. Wonderful." I stepped in closer, "I hope that curry tastes as good as it smells."

His dimples deepened. "Good thing I showed up without the mask."

It was immediately obvious that both of us had been looking forward to the warmth that kiss brought for some time. The combination of soft lips, strong arms wrapped in flannel, and the deep stir of cloves and cardamom made it feel like my winter had finally ended.

"It's good. Sweet," I whispered as I separated my lips from his, a hint of coconut lingering on his breath.

"I thought we'd have less 'burn' and more 'learn' tonight," he whispered back, going in for a deeper kiss.

And there I was, just like that first day, holding onto Alex for dear life. But this was a much more pleasant fall. No banged-up knees, no awkward apologies, no bitter chill, and all smiles out in the open. He simply strung my arm through his and we walked off the platform into the mild spring air, on our way—finally—to our shared destination. ♥

UNRAVEL

♥ *by Charlie Gallows*

The spring-loaded door slams shut behind him, muting the noisy city street with a *bang*.

Diego searches the sparsely populated bar for a familiar face—*the* familiar face, actually, *her* face—but he only finds strangers.

Fuck.

Grinding his molars, he starts towards a vacant swath of bar top by the jukebox at the opposite end of the room.

Something about this place unnerves him.

The sloped floor and low ceiling create a kind of funhouse effect, cautioning uncertainty with each step. In lieu of overhead lighting, neon beer signs catch every glossy surface, all the vinyl upholstery and heavily-lacquered wood lending the atmosphere a dim, red pulse.

Sunglasses don't help alleviate the distortion. Tinted lenses morph shadows into chasms that he hesitates to approach. But according to Sav, his eyes give everything away, and she's probably right.

Each of these factors plays their own part in the symphony stripping his nerves raw, but none so loud as the simple fact that he's never been here without her.

As he takes a seat at the bar, the jukebox behind him kicks to life and starts blasting Warhol-era art rock. All brash sincerity and understated talent, it complements the venue in a strange way. Like the music always belonged here, so integral to the lopsided foundation that its absence is jarring. Without it, the place is just a poorly-maintained basement with shitty lighting. But with it? *It's fucking underground, baby.*

The bartender places a coaster in front of him. "Whiskey, neat, right?"

"Yeah." Diego checks his watch, "Make it a double?"

"Double, you got it."

While the bartender pours his drink, Diego anchors his gaze to the door, wringing his hands absentmindedly. He stares for so long his vision blurs into abstract, the exit sign melting down to a vague red glow as his stomach twists in knots.

"Where's Van?"

Ripping his attention away from the door, Diego raises his eyebrows. "Hmm?"

"You usually come here with Van, right?" the bartender asks.

"Oh—*Van*, Savannah. Yeah."

Just her name on his tongue makes him tingle. *Fuck*, this is bad.

"She's cool." The bartender sets Diego's drink down on the coaster, nodding casually. "Stops by every couple of days, sweet girl." He frowns, "Are you two...?"

"No," Diego snorts and digs out his wallet, shaking his head. "No, we are not... *that*. We're—well, we're friends. Honestly, she's closer to a wingman than a girlfriend."

He winces at his own clumsy overcorrection. It doesn't matter past the first word anyway. The bartender scans the room until Diego stops rambling, then plows ahead.

"Right on, right on. So, what's her deal then, is she single?"

"Far as I know," he shrugs, studying the bartender over the rim of his sunglasses. He tosses some cash on the rail. "Keep the change."

"Thanks for the tip," the bartender raps a knuckle on the bar top, scooping up the money on his way to the register.

What Diego wants to say is, "*Here's a tip: don't fucking look at her,*" but he doesn't have the right. Instead, he rolls his eyes behind the privacy of dark lenses, then takes a big swallow of whiskey. It burns the whole way down, settling warm in his belly.

He checks his watch and allows his gaze to drift back to the door. He stares at it and drinks and wonders what he'll do if or when she doesn't show. Drink some more, probably. Drown the bruised pit in his chest until he can't feel it anymore.

They knew what they were getting into by going home with that guy from the bar. Diego knew, at least. And wasn't she the one to talk him into it?

Maybe he should have said no.

Fuck, how could he?

Especially when she was looking at him that way she does sometimes. With heavy lids and big doe eyes, all hopeful and sparkling and easily distracted by his mouth. He could swear he heard her whispered desire, but can't trust his own ears.

Alcohol seeps into his bloodstream, melting his stiff muscles. He brings the glass to his lips again and again and again, waxing and waning with each sip.

Maybe he should count his blessings.

If it were up to him, this would've happened well before they established this weekly tradition of loose inhibitions. Minus the third party and all the dramatics, ideally, but beggars can't be choosers.

Doesn't she know by now that he'd never refuse her?

Maybe she shouldn't have asked him.

It's *her* goddamn ethos. No strings means no ties to cut, means no hurt feelings. Leave before the sun goes up and never look back.

So of course, they got along. They just had to vibrate at the exact same goddamn frequency. By the time he propositioned her, she had to decline.

'Too stringy,' she said, *'I like you too much.'*

Maybe he should have asked what she meant by that.

He checks his watch. Ten minutes late. Static rises in his chest, crackling through his fingertips. What if she doesn't show?

Maybe he should leave and never look back.

He takes another sip only to find an empty glass at his lips. A sign he should go.

Right?

Just as he frowns with indecision, daylight pours in from the street, and a familiar face—*the* familiar face, *her* face—walks through the door.

His heart swells when he sees her.

Of course she looks like a goddamn knockout. Wearing this little black slip of a dress that clings to her curves. All dolled up with loose, dark curls spilling over her shoulders. Her magnetic presence straightens him to attention.

When she spots Diego, her whole face brightens, warming him the way whiskey never could.

She stops to give the starry-eyed bartender her order, pointing to Diego and nodding, then comes over and hops up on the barstool beside him. Something about her scent, salon-brand shampoo laced with her summer musk, causes him to salivate.

He clears his throat and swallows, then looks over at her, "Hey."

"Hey, sorry I'm late. I, umm..." Her mouth opens, but all that comes out is a nervous chuckle before it snaps shut. She tucks her hair behind her ear and shrugs, avoiding his gaze, "I don't know. Sorry."

Diego waves off her apology and leans forward against the bar, watching the bartender mix her drink a few feet away. Within his earshot, neither of them makes an attempt to open Pandora's invisible box. Dead-weight silence hangs in the air between them, not so much a stalemate or a lull as a tongue stained with bite marks.

When the bartender delivers a dirty martini to Sav, he accepts her credit card. "Opening a tab?"

"Umm..." She frowns and glances at Diego, who shrugs, then mimics the action to the bartender.

"Sure, yeah." Pointing to Diego's empty glass, she asks, "Can we get another one of these, too?"

"You got it, sweetheart." He taps her credit card against the bar and turns away.

Sav sips while Diego wrings his hands and fidgets and stares at his empty glass. Its former contents slosh fuzzily through his veins.

Every so often he steals glances of her, catching some of the little things that paint a bigger picture. Fingernails gnawed down to ragged edges. Raw, chapped lips. These subtle, nervous jaw movements like she's chewing on the soft bits of her mouth.

'I'm no good at keeping secrets,' she once told him. *'They eat away at me.'*

"Double bourbon, neat." The bartender replaces his empty glass with one filled two-thirds, then looks between them, "Anything else for you two?"

"No, thank you." Sav flashes him that polite smile that really means *please fuck off*, and he does just that. As soon as he's gone, Sav leans back in her chair and stares at Diego.

She asks, "Are you stoned or something?"

"No, why?"

"Because you're wearing sunglasses and it's like a fucking dungeon in here?"

He frowns and shakes his head, "I'm not stoned. A little buzzed, but not stoned."

"Okay, well... Should we talk about it?"

"Do you wanna talk about it?"

"Well yeah, I wouldn't be here if I didn't," she scoffs, sitting up to trace the rim of her martini glass. "But, I guess you wouldn't be either, so..."

Her implication hangs in the air for a moment before he admits, "I'm surprised you showed up."

"Of course I did, why wouldn't I?"

He snorts and shakes his head as if to say, *You know damn well why.*

She takes a sip of her martini, then shrugs. "I'm surprised I showed up, too, if I'm being honest. I wasn't sure if I wanted to or not. I went on a walk to think it over and, umm... Well, I wound up here, so... I guess I did."

When she lifts her gaze to study him, heat percolates at his middle. All he can think about is how her mouth tasted. How her cunt tasted. How fucking good her skin felt against his, back pressed to his chest as she gasped curse-filled praises in his ear.

"Will you take them off?" She gestures at his sunglasses. "I just, um..." Her tongue peeks out to wet her lips, and she shrugs, confessing in a quiet voice, "I don't know... I just need to see you."

He opens his mouth to refuse, until he sees the dewy earnestness written on her face. His chest aches and his stomach flutters and he understands suddenly that she could ask him for the moon and he'd deliver it at her feet, consequences be damned.

Diego takes off the glasses and sets them on the bar top, blinking at her. "Better?"

She nods, barely suppressing a smile.

Light flickers through him when their eyes meet, unhindered. As if shocked by the same jolt, she looks away and chews her lower lip. The shine of her saliva catches his eye. He wants to lick it off.

"How long were you waiting for me?" she asks.

All my life.

"Not long. Five, ten minutes."

"Mmm," she hums, mid-sip, then sets her glass down and fiddles with the stem. "Okay, and, umm... just curious—how many times did you think about running out the door?"

"Only about a thousand." He grins at her so she knows it's a joke. Sort of, kind of.

"Impressive," she chuckles and tilts her head at him. "But here you are."

He holds eye contact despite the flames licking away at his insides. "Here I am."

Alarms sound at the back of his head as she reads his face, but all he can seem to focus on is how fucking *beautiful* she is. All her freckles and fine lines. The red neon glow catching her cheekbone and the slope of her nose. Her pillowy lips all plumped up from anxiety-induced auto cannibalism.

Averting her gaze to her drink, she leads, "So... how do you wanna do this?"

Diego leans back in his barstool, crossing his arms over his chest with a shrug. "I'm open to suggestions."

"Well, umm... hang on, let me just—" She raises the martini glass to her lips and tips it back. Her whole face twists into a wince when she sets it down, shuddering. "*Fuck*—nope, bad idea."

He snorts and shakes his head as she plucks a big green olive from the grave of her martini and pops it into her mouth, then swivels to face him.

"Okay, let's see…"

Eyes still watery from vodka burn, she starts doing that thing she does when she brainstorms, turning her wrists in loose circles, wiggling in her seat while she searches the ceiling for answers. "We could totally backpedal, drink ourselves blind and shove our feelings like way, *way* down, and never speak of this again."

"A classic," he nods, playing along despite his clenching stomach.

"We could sort of take turns," she says. "Do some Q and A. We could, you know, um… open up a word vomitorium, just fuckin', I don't know—spill our guts all over the place."

She tilts her head from side to side, considering. "*Or!* Or, we could workshop this new bit I've been working on for my routine. It's about the mortifying consequences of having a three-way with some rando and my closest friend—unrelated, of course."

"Oh, of course."

Their eyes meet. They both crack, smiles spreading across their faces, releasing the smallest amount of pressure from their bubble of conversation.

A beat of silence goes by before Diego clears his throat and finds the courage to ask, "Why did you ask me?"

"Ask you what?"

He blinks at her and she just blinks back, oblivious.

Shaking his head, he clarifies, "Why'd you ask me to be your third?"

"Oh–*duh*. Fuck, okay." She draws a sharp breath and nods, then leans in, lowering her voice, "Okay. Well. I've always wanted to, you know..."

"Get double stuffed?"

"Wow, what a gentleman," she snorts. "Thanks, yeah. *'Double stuffed.'* And... well, I don't know. It's sort of fuzzy. But I told him that, and—"

"You told him you've always wanted to take two dicks at the same time?"

She blinks at him. "Yeah, so?"

"Incredible," he chuckles.

"What?"

"Nothing, you're just..." He glances over at her and shakes his head. "Never mind. So, what, you told him that, and...?"

Inspecting her hands, she shrugs, pitching her voice high. "And... I don't know. He said he was down, and you were right there at the bar, so... yeah.

I asked you."

He stares at her, giving her a chance to speak her entire truth, but she becomes so preoccupied with a frayed thumbnail that she doesn't notice. Picking and biting, fully distracted.

Amazing. A modern-day Pinocchio, so haunted by her days as a marionette that the sight of strings makes her queasy. Instead of having a nose that grows, she needs to chip away at herself every time she lies.

With a sigh, Diego digs his multi-tool pocket knife from his pants pocket and pops the nail file into action mode.

He swivels the barstool to face her and motions for her hand. "Here, let me see."

"Hmm?" She raises her eyebrows at him in question, then seems to realize what he's asking of her. "*Oh*, you don't have to. I mean, I can—"

"Christ, Bambi, how many times have I done this for you? It's not a big deal."

She huffs and rolls her eyes, but holds her hand out to him.

He takes it in his to examine the offending nail, trying not to dwell on how warm and soft her skin feels.

As he goes to work grinding down the jagged edge, he asks, "Do you remember when we met?"

"Mmm, the worst day of my life? Yeah, I remember." Her eyes catch his when he glances up at her, and she quickly adds, "Not because of *you* or anything. I was talking about the, umm—well, you know..."

"The mandatory seventy-two hour psych hold?"

"That's the one."

He nods, smoothing the pad of his thumb against the rough grain of her nail. "All through breakfast, the hens were clucking about a new girl. Just as we started clearing out to get ready for morning group, you came into the commons. I remember you standing there, all wide-eyed and skittish, trying to figure out where to sit. You were holding a cafeteria tray with just this apple on it, and the apple was sort of wobbling back and forth because your hands were so damn shaky."

"Yeah, I'm a shitshow. What's your point, Dee?"

"I'm getting there."

With a huff, she pulls her hand away and checks her surroundings, then tucks some hair behind her ear. "I don't like talking about it. I don't... I don't *like* that part of me."

Heavy solemnity seems to overcome her—shoulders slumped, gaze downcast and distant. It echoes inside him and pulls his heartstrings taut.

He sits up, looking around as he folds the nail file away in his pocket. When he leans forward and plucks her hands off her lap, they sort of wilt in his while he stares at her, waiting for a reaction.

"Savannah."

"What?"

"Look at me, doll."

Childlike irritation flashes through her eyes as they meet his.

He promises, "I'm getting there."

She sighs, searching his face. Then, slowly but surely, the heat of her impatience dissolves to a warm, steady thrum.

"Fine," she concedes, rolling her eyes a little. "You better have a point though."

"I swear, I do."

After taking a deep breath, she prompts, "So, there I was, the most pathetic girl in the world..."

"Most pathetic girl in the world," he snorts and shakes his head. "You were a strong contender in that moment, if we're being honest."

"Rude ass," she swats at him playfully.

He grins at her, dropping his gaze when her hand returns to his.

"No, but, uhh..." His thumb brushes up against her knuckles and he clears his throat, raising his eyes to hers.

"There you were, a deer in headlights with your wobbly apple, freshly institutionalized, and umm... Well, once I picked my jaw up off the floor—because *Jesus Christ*, look at you—this thought popped in my head."

He chuckles, "I should probably lie and say something like, *'The first time I saw you, I heard angels singing,'* or whatever the fuck, but, uhh... if we're being honest, when I saw you I distinctly remember thinking: *'I want to see her unravel.'*"

She tilts her head, squinting at him as her mouth silently traces the word—*unravel.* Then she asks, "What the fuck does that mean?"

"I don't know. I *didn't* know. But I think it's starting to make more sense because, well... Since then, I've seen you fall apart in so many ways. From grief and anger and pleasure and joy. You are so... *raw* in your emotions."

He takes a moment to contemplate the accuracy of this statement, then nods, "Raw and messy and, *fuck*—so beautiful. I adore that about you. Really, I do."

Her big brown eyes search his face, wide and vulnerable.

"What I mean is that I've *seen* you, Sav. At your worst and at your best. And I see you now, and I'm still right here. So... be honest, you know? Tell me about the apple wobbling around in your head."

She continues to stare at him for a few seconds before looking down at their clasped hands and smirking. "You really wanna know why I asked you?"

Half-strangled by his heart, he croaks, "I really do."

"Okay, well... I guess if we're being honest, I did want to try the—" She cuts herself off with a sharp laugh, then clears her throat and grins, "The '*double stuffing.*' But mostly I asked you to join because, I, umm... I wanted to try... you?"

Her glossy eyes flick all over his face, and she adds softly, "Is that bad?"

"Is it *bad?*"

Biting back a smile, she shrugs.

"Christ, Bambi—no, not at all. Seriously. *Bad?* Fuck no," he scoffs and shakes his head, "For the record, I'm not the one who had objections to us hooking up, whether it was a three-way or anything else. That was all you, doll. '*Too stringy*'—that's what you said."

The sinful red glow of neon across her skin deepens a shade as she glances away. "I know."

These two words hold weight, but sound more like a fraction than a whole thought. He scoots his stool closer, slotting her knees between his.

When he cups her cheek, she melts against his palm, heavy-lidded gaze drifting between his eyes and mouth. Something warm gives way between them and swells at the base of his spine.

"It *is* too stringy," she shrugs, watching his hand drop to her bare leg. As she speaks, his fingertips explore her skin. He scrawls tiny hearts and valentines just for her.

"I don't know, Dee. You're my favorite person, pretty much my best friend. But, umm... if we're being honest, I can't stop thinking about it. Fucking you, I mean. It was..." She sort of holds her breath, then chuckles, "Well, you were there."

Pride swells in his chest, burning up his neck. He writes *BE MINE* on her knee and grins, "It *was* fucking hot, right?"

"Yeah, umm..." Laughter bubbles up her throat, and she covers her face, "I don't think I've ever come that hard in my fucking life, it was—" She fans herself. "Sorry, um, yeah. Agreed."

He writes *KISS ME* at the hem of her dress and she fixates on his mouth like she's actually considering it.

"Honestly, though..." She shakes her head, still staring at his lips. "My stomach does a flippy thing every time I see you. And when I think about how bad you could hurt me if you wanted to—"

Her eyes take on water as she searches his face, voice trembling as she admits, "It scares the shit out of me, Diego."

It feels a little like toeing the edge of a cliff when he clears his throat in preparation to speak, all stomach lurch and vertigo, but he takes the next step anyway.

"I'm scared, too," he husks, holding her gaze so she'll know he means it. "You know, I did actually consider running. Before you got here, I mean. But it was only because... well, I thought if I left before it was obvious you weren't gonna show, I'd never have to know you didn't want this."

He brushes his knuckles across her knee and shrugs. "But I'd never know if you *did* want this, either, so... I don't know. I almost ran, but I didn't."

"I'm glad you didn't."

"So am I," he murmurs, scrawling *TRUE LOVE* on her soft inner thigh.

The contact makes her shiver, her dark eyes going all hot and gooey. A small whine escapes her lips and she spreads her legs wide enough so he can feel heat radiate from between them. Every cell in his body aches with want.

She tugs on his shirt, glancing at his mouth. He slips his hand around her waist, and she bows towards him, so perfect and warm that nothing else matters. Not a single fucking thing.

The bar could be burning down around them and he wouldn't have a clue because she's draping her arms over his shoulders, combing her fingers through his curls and looking at him that way she does, all doe-eyed and leaning in just so he can taste the vodka on her breath and—

He presses his lips to hers.

When she pulls him closer, deepening the kiss, everything else ceases to exist. The entire universe melts down to a pinhole. Just the wet roll of her tongue. The taste of her spit. How fucking soft and hot her mouth feels. How she lets out these sweet, breathy whines every time their lips part and reconnect like she needs this as much as he does.

All the while, this heady, intoxicating sensation wells up inside him. It bangs on the walls of his heart and strips him threadbare. It reduces him down to heat and magic and the absolute truth that he is ruined for anything but this.

Anyone but *her* would be a lie.

Diego pulls back enough to meet her gaze, but not so far that he loses the heat of her breath. He searches her face, grazing her jawline en route to her cheek.

Her lashes flutter at the contact. She leans into his palm, eyes sparkling as they flick around his face. This big luminescent smile spreads across her face, casting light on everything he's ever known.

"What?" he chuckles.

"Nothing, you just..." Still grinning, she glances at his mouth. "You keep looking at me like that."

"Like what?"

"Like you think the sun shines out of my ass."

"Doesn't it?" he implores.

"You would know," Sav smirks, reaching up to

hold his palm to her cheek.

Lacing his fingers with hers, he pulls her hand to his lips and murmurs, "I would, wouldn't I?" then presses a kiss into each of her knuckles. Every peck echoes across her features in needy little flashes.

She slips from his grip to rub the pad of her thumb across his bottom lip. Desire pulses through him, thick and hot and disastrous.

Her eyes light up when he stifles a moan. She feeds him more. He graciously accepts, relishing the scrape of her fingerprint on his tongue.

"Oh my *god*, Dee—"

Someone in an alternate universe clears his stupid throat and catapults them back to Earth. "*Ahem.*"

They startle on impact, pulling away from each other to look at the intrusion.

"Do guys mind taking this somewhere else?" The bartender nods over his shoulder, as if speaking on behalf of the disinterested patrons behind him. "You're making people uncomfortable."

"People, or just you?" Diego mutters, earning a leveled stare from the bartender.

Covering a giggle, Sav swats his shoulder, then swivels her stool to face the bar.

"Sorry, umm... yeah. Let me just close—"

The bartender sets down a pen and receipt, making a point to roll his eyes before shoving off to the other end of the bar.

"Oh—wow, okay," she snorts, and glances over at Diego while filling in blanks on the slip of curled-up paper. "So... What now? Do you wanna go to my place, or...?"

"I thought you'd never ask."

She grins at him before dropping her gaze to his mouth, drawing him in for another kiss. Her lips meet his, hungry but patient, ripe with the same certainty he feels bone-deep.

Rising to his feet, Diego tosses a few dollars down on the bar, then offers Savannah a hand. Lacing their fingers together, she hops down off the stool and leads him towards the entrance.

"Better luck next time!" he calls over his shoulder to the bartender as daylight pours in from the street.

Sav yanks him along, half-groaning, half-laughing. "Oh my *god*, we're never coming back here."

They wander out into the sunshine, fingers entwined, hearts beating in sync. The spring-loaded door slams shut behind them with a *bang*, but neither one of them hears it. ♥

PROVE IT

♥ *by Jayce Hanna*

Tobias winced at the sound of the front door flying open. It *banged* off the side of the house and echoed like a gunshot, disturbing the stillness of the empty street with its well-manicured lawns, expensive cars, and large houses whose sleeping residents surely dreamt of nothing worse than social faux pas and unpolished silverware.

Although he hadn't been the one to fling the door open, Tobias was embarrassed at being involved in such a ruckus. This was *not* the kind of neighborhood where people shouted or slammed doors in the middle of the night.

His embarrassment flared higher as he was unceremoniously shoved outside, desperately trying— and failing—to keep both his balance and his dignity.

Tobias's knees hit the pavement hard, but he bit his tongue and kept from crying out as he quickly scrambled to his feet.

"Get the *fuck* out of my house!" The voice behind him was decibels louder than what was appropriate for the late hour, and vibrated with rage.

Unfounded rage, no less! People could be such fucking babies sometimes when they didn't get exactly what they wanted.

Tobias had been nothing but upfront about the conditions for this arrangement right from the start, just like he'd been with all the others. He was a temporary thing, he always told them. Theirs for a short while before it was time to part ways.

It wasn't his fault that some of them just didn't listen when he explained that his heart wasn't on the table. Not his fault that, despite this caveat, some people had the audacity to think they would be the exception.

As if that role hadn't already been cast, years prior.

"Gladly!" he hissed back, then quickly dodged as one of his shoes came whirling past his left ear.

"You think you're gonna do better than this? Huh?" the man sneered. "You think people don't smell the street on you? Beneath those pretty clothes and jewelry, you're still just a rat."

Tobias didn't dignify that with a response, just raised his middle finger before turning around. He violently regretted ever telling this man anything about his past. Usually, Tobias prided himself on being a good judge of character, but clearly he'd been swayed by green eyes and a smile that he was just pathetic enough to admit had reminded him of someone else.

The other shoe hit him square in the back a second later, no doubt leaving a stain on his half-buttoned white satin shirt. It didn't matter. At least this way he wouldn't have to walk barefoot.

The door slammed shut behind him again and Tobias picked up his shoes, straightened his back, and started walking. He was certain that, by now, at least a few of the nosy neighbors had made it over to their windows, and he refused to give them even more of a show.

To add insult to injury, it started raining a few minutes later.

Tobias stopped a couple of streets over to put his shoes on and finish buttoning up his shirt, but that did little to keep the cold at bay. The rain had seeped through the thin shirt in seconds, chilling him to the bone and making his teeth chatter, like a rattlesnake coiled in his mouth.

Tobias really hated the rain.

Thankfully, he didn't need to walk for long before approaching his destination. Tonight, he wasn't heading towards his own meager apartment. *That* lay on the other side of the city, and not even his fuming indignation over having been kicked out like a discarded toy would have kept him warm enough to make that trip on foot.

Tonight, Tobias was headed towards a home that wasn't his—but it had always felt like it, solely thanks to the man who lived there.

He'd been there too many times to count, but usually during daylight, and Tobias felt a twinge of guilt over showing up in the middle of the night like this.

A small candle-flame of hope flickered to life in his chest and snuffed out most of the guilt, however, as he saw lights through the windows, signaling that someone was home and still awake. Tobias let out a shuddering breath he hadn't been aware of holding.

Moving up the stone steps, pride made him hesitate when he reached the top stair and caught sight of his reflection in the narrow glass panes of the door. His usually lush chestnut locks lay plastered against his forehead like a dripping helmet and his posture, hunched against the cold, really wasn't doing him any favors. It was pathetic enough to show up here so late at night. He didn't have to emphasize the wretched orphan effect.

Forcing his frozen muscles into action to straighten his spine, Tobias ran his hand through his hair, mussing up the locks into something more playful. He faked a smile and willed his appearance more into that of a water nymph than a drenched rat before he knocked.

A few moments later, the door opened slowly, and cautious green eyes behind wire-rimmed glasses met his, widening in surprise and recognition.

"Tobias?"

The worry in the soft familiar voice almost broke through his defenses and did him in, but Tobias was nothing if not a showman. He couldn't hide the chattering of his teeth, but his smile barely wavered as he cocked his hip to lean casually against the stair railing.

"Patrick, darling. F-fancy a drink?"

Caught off guard, either by Tobias's question or appearance, Patrick's face paraded through a series of unidentifiable expressions as he considered the best way to proceed. Tonight, the risk of Tobias catching hypothermia on his doorstep seemed to win out over any desire for immediate clarity regarding the reason for the visit, and Patrick simply took a step to the side to let him in.

Tobias loved when their priorities aligned.

Tobias, in fact, loved many things about Patrick—most things, really—but Patrick also seemed to be completely immune to Tobias's charm and flirtation, and very oblivious to the fact that he had been gifted Tobias's heart regardless.

He'd never outright turned Tobias down. Perhaps because Tobias had never outright *asked*, preferring to skirt the line of plausible deniability should Patrick actually call him out. Their friendship was too important for Tobias to risk by doing more than harmlessly flirt.

Because above all else, Patrick was a good and kind man, so stratospherically out of his league that even Tobias's masochistic tendencies begged him sometimes to dial down the unrequited affection to more tolerable levels. He'd happily settle for platonic smiles and affections if that meant he got to stay in Patrick's orbit.

"L-lovely evening, w-wouldn't you say?" Tobias brushed past Patrick with a smirk, the effect of it somewhat lessened by the way he was still shivering.

He gave Patrick a once-over. His friend looked unfairly good in his ugly beige pajamas. Soft, and huggable enough that Tobias had to clench his fists so that he wouldn't do something stupid.

"Where is your coat?" Patrick asked, as if Tobias hadn't spoken at all. His eyes were glued somewhere in the vicinity of Tobias's nipples. The— by now—translucent shirt did nothing to obscure them.

But Tobias didn't let himself get his hopes up. There was not an inkling of heat in Patrick's gaze.

Just worry with a hint of disapproval, as if Tobias's coatless state was a deliberate fashion statement.

"Oh let's s-see... last time I s-saw it, I believe it was it was thrown over the b-back of a couch. Not entirely s-sure. The brain gets m-muddled in the throes of passion, after all." He grinned and waggled his eyebrows suggestively.

Patrick looked wholly unimpressed by everything coming out of Tobias's mouth.

"It's October!"

"Time f-flies, doesn't it? S-say do you have any p-plans for—"

"*Tobias!*" There was just enough steel in Patrick's voice that Tobias fell silent. "Enough of this act. What. *Happened?*"

Tobias lowered his gaze, unequipped to deal with the genuine concern he could hear in Patrick's voice. How many other people showed him such care? The list was depressingly short.

"I was th-thrown out," he confessed, quietly.

Patrick didn't immediately respond, and Tobias was just on the verge of bolting when a warm hand closed around his wrist.

"Come on, let's get you some tea and warm clothes. I can't fucking *believe* he threw you out in the middle of the night without your coat." Patrick sounded angry, his voice in sharp contrast to the gentle grip of his fingers as he led Tobias to the warm, cozy kitchen.

"Not every f-frog you kiss can be a p-prince charming in d-disguise, I guess," Tobias replied, going for lighthearted and casual, but landing somewhere closer to disappointed and hurt.

Patrick's expression softened. "Well, have you considered... not kissing frogs?"

Tobias had, in fact, considered it. Many times. But he didn't tell Patrick that. Instead, he just followed him into the apartment in silent gratitude.

* * *

Tobias was rarely the sentimental type—genuine feelings were mushy and messy at the best of times and seldom lived up to their hype—but something complicated was going on in his chest. He stood in the guest room, a big towel wrapped around his shoulders like a cape and a steaming mug of tea clasped in his hands while he watched the kind man in the ugly beige pajamas spread an extra blanket over the bed and lay out another pair of equally ugly pajamas for Tobias to borrow.

No one did this. Not for him. If Tobias was given clothes, it was because they would make him look good enough to drool over. No one dressed him for comfort and warmth. No one, except...

"Marry me," he mumbled and Patrick looked over

at him with one of those infuriatingly soft smiles. His eyes twinkled in the dim light, putting all the gemstones of the world to shame, and for a moment Tobias felt like the richest man alive, being on the receiving end of that look.

"I hear your tongue has thawed, but I think your brain might still need some time to catch up before it's back to being fully operational," Patrick teased.

It really was incredibly inconvenient that Tobias's heart insisted on carrying a torch for a man who had no interest in him.

It had been inconvenient at fourteen when Patrick had confided in him that there was someone he wanted to kiss and Tobias, in a jealous fit, had declared that kissing was *so* disgusting, which made Patrick never bring the subject up again.

It had been equally inconvenient at eighteen when Patrick was going off to a college Tobias hadn't been smart enough to get into. Patrick had asked him to come along, regardless, but Tobias had said no. At this age, he had still been holding onto the hope of falling in love with someone else— mainly the guy he'd been sorta dating for the past month. But Tobias didn't fall in love with him, and they broke up four days after Patrick left because Tobias wouldn't stop crying.

He took another sip from the mug of steaming hot tea and relished the burn in his throat and its valiant attempt to cover up the sting of rejection. So fucking inconvenient.

* * *

An hour later, Tobias was slowly realizing that despite the weary feeling of his limbs, sleep would probably be a no-go. The blanket and pajamas, soft as the man they belonged to, were just as comfortable as the other few times he'd spent the night here, but tonight Tobias just felt *cold*. He wasn't used to sleeping by himself, and the room felt too big and too quiet without another person there to keep him grounded.

Tobias's brain, of course, wasted no time in providing a solution to this problem, and while his sense of shame and dignity tried to appeal to reason, the protests were weak and easily pushed aside.

So, Tobias slid out of bed and carefully tiptoed across the hallway to knock gently on Patrick's door, pushing it open just as the other man stirred.

Patrick's hair stuck up in all directions as he lifted his head from the pillow, squinting at Tobias to compensate for the lack of his glasses.

"Tobias? Is everything okay?" Patrick asked, in a sleep-rough voice that had no business sounding like *that*.

"I'm cold," Tobias complained, voice petulant

and whiny to hide the effect Patrick's voice was having on the stability of both his knees and his sanity.

Patrick rubbed his eyes. "I'm sorry, Tobias, I would change the weather for you if I could, but I'm afraid it's beyond my control. But if you—"

"Can I stay with you?" Tobias interrupted before he had time to chicken out. Begging for company should have been beneath him, but he really didn't want to spend the night alone.

Patrick stilled. When he spoke there was a slight waver to his voice. "Do you think that's wise?" (As if Tobias had ever made his decisions based on what was considered wise.)

"I think it beats dying in your guest room."

"You're not going to die in the guest room, Tobias."

"I might!"

Patrick didn't argue any further. Instead, he scooted over slightly to one side and lifted the edge of the sheets just enough for Tobias to recognize the invitation.

The bed was warm when he laid down, and Tobias stretched like a cat finding a particularly pleasant spot in the sun as he relaxed into the sheets with a soft moan.

Patrick, however, seemed to have lost hold of whatever relaxation sleep had previously provided.

It didn't take a genius to figure out the cause.

"Look at you," Tobias teased, "Clutching that blanket like a blushing virgin. Are you afraid I'll take advantage of you?"

"That's not what I—" Patrick sighed, but he did relax just a fraction. "I'm sorry."

"Don't beat yourself up too much, I was actually thinking about how I could best manipulate you into holding me. I am still a bit cold."

It was mostly a joke. Tobias didn't want to push for more than what was offered, but Patrick was so entertaining to tease. There was a small wrinkle of a frown that always appeared whenever Tobias nudged the boundary of their friendship just a little out of Patrick's comfort zone, and an addictive intensity to his gaze when he studied Tobias— no doubt to assess whether the teasing actually warranted a response.

Tobias could bask in that gaze forever, but at the same time, he was terrified of pushing too far and seeing that hint of a frown turn into full-blown disapproval. So he watered down what he really wanted to say, held most of it back, and pretended that the truth was nothing but jokes and good-natured teasing.

Silence hung in the air between them after To-bias's comment, and when he finally gave in and turned his head a fraction to glance at Patrick, he found the other man watching him with that little frown and some mixture of disbelief and awe.

"You're unbelievable."

"Thank you," Tobias grinned.

"You seem awfully sure that was a compliment," Patrick tossed back.

"Wasn't it?"

Patrick let out a soft laugh. "Yeah... yeah, it was."

Tobias smiled and found the expression mirrored on Patrick's face in the near-dark.

"This is the first time you've asked to stay in my bed," Patrick mused, as if the realization had just struck him. He shifted a little closer to Tobias's side of the bed.

"Funny what almost perishing from hypothermia will do to you," Tobias joked.

Suddenly, he was very aware of the proximity between their faces. Surely, Patrick's eyesight wasn't bad enough that he had to be that close? Patrick's lips were slightly parted and Tobias felt the soft exhales against his own, scented with the faint, minty traces of toothpaste.

For a few trembling moments, Tobias could have sworn that time stopped. Patrick was watching him, pupils blown so wide that the irises were barely visible, and Tobias felt seen, almost to the point of discomfort.

Make a joke, his brain shouted. *Lighten the mood*

before you say something stupid like telling him you love him!

But before Tobias's frozen mouth could comply with his brain's orders, Patrick spoke.

"Are you really still cold?" he asked.

"Yes," Tobias replied. He kind of was, and agreeing seemed to be the route towards safer interactions than staring into Patrick's eyes until he saw a mirage of feelings there.

Patrick closed his mouth and nodded, a determined set to his jaw. Tobias expected him to offer another blanket, fetch another mug of tea, or light the fireplace. What he didn't expect was for Patrick to scoot closer and slide his arm around Tobias's waist, and gently tug him against his chest.

For a moment, surprise stunned Tobias out of protesting as his head was carefully tucked under Patrick's chin—oh *gods*, he smelled good!—and Tobias felt as if he'd accidentally skipped several steps on his way down the stairs, or fallen into an alternate reality without noticing. Because there was 'being oblivious to the effect you had on other people,' and then there was whatever the hell Patrick was currently doing.

When Tobias regained control of his faculties, he pulled back, almost afraid to look directly at the impostor who had clearly taken over Patrick's body.

"What... what is going on here?" Tobias hated

how weak and unsure he sounded.

But of course, Patrick noticed. "Is something wrong? You don't like being held?"

"I like it just fine, but..."

"But...?"

Tobias floundered, thoughts moving too quickly and not quite settling into anything coherent.

"Holding a man in your bed like this could give him ideas!" he finally blurted, realizing as he said it that the words could be interpreted both as a warning and a confession.

Patrick, the bastard, had the audacity to blush.

"I don't mind," he said after a moment's hesitation. "I mean, after all... it would be quite disheartening if this inspired nothing whatsoever."

Tobias was sure he must have misheard him. Or perhaps he had actually died from hypothermia in Patrick's guest room and this was just the last huzzah of his imagination before the afterlife claimed him.

He stared at Patrick, unblinking.

"Tobias?" Patrick said gently. "Are you—"

"But you're not attracted to me!" Tobias blurted out, as if reminding the universe of this indisputable truth would suddenly make the situation revert back to something that made sense.

Patrick frowned, biting his cheek the way Tobias knew he only did when he was nervous. "What if I am?" There was the faintest hint of a challenge to his tone. "What if I'm attracted to you?"

Tobias let out a laugh that sounded unhinged, even to his own ears. He opened his mouth to answer, then closed it again because Patrick was watching him and, even if Tobias didn't dare to interpret it, the expression on his face was genuine.

"Prove it!" Tobias demanded, his last ounce of sanity exiting the building.

"What?"

"If you're attracted to me, then prove it!"

Patrick gazed at Tobias, his face rotating through the same series of unidentifiable expressions as it had when Tobias first showed up. Then it settled into something utterly terrifying—terrifying because it made hope flicker in Tobias's chest.

A second later, Patrick's fingers brushed against his cheek and Tobias shot back, "What are you doing?"

"Oh for Heaven's—would you just hold still," Patrick said, closing the distance between them.

His lips were warm and soft, everything Tobias had imagined them to be. Gentle at first, giving Tobias plenty of time to pull back, as if this wasn't the one thing Tobias had truly wanted since he was old enough to realize that he was hopelessly in love with his best friend.

It took a barely-there nudge of Patrick's tongue

against the seam of his lips for Tobias's body to finally get with the program.

As he surged forward, forcing a surprised sound from Patrick's mouth, Tobias had the fleeting thought that this had better be real, because he would not survive if he blinked his eyes and found himself back in the cold guest room again.

So he *grabbed* Patrick, fingers clutching at the front of his pajamas to pull him closer, at the same time that Patrick's arm tightened around his waist. Like two magnets finally snapping together, they kissed, unable to resist the pull for another second.

The next kiss they shared wasted no time moving from sweet and chaste to desperate and dizzying, and Tobias had zero complaints about that. Four hands tugged urgently to get their meddlesome shirts out of the way, granting easier access for greedy fingers to explore.

Tobias had seen Patrick without his shirt several times, but touching was a whole different ballpark. He'd known what the scar on Patrick's shoulder looked like, a souvenir from a bicycle accident when they were seventeen. Now, Tobias traced it with his fingers like he was reading a little snippet of their shared history in Braille.

For his part, Patrick's hand was spread across Tobias's ribs, partially covering the tattoo that he had helped Tobias choose the day he'd finally moved out of his parents' house.

Through touch, they were rediscovering things they already knew about each other's bodies, but the experience felt brand-new.

They were *kissing.* And if the hard line pressed against Tobias's thigh was anything to go by, Patrick found the experience just as exciting as he did.

"I thought you were immune to my flirting," Tobias mumbled against Patrick's lips. He felt drunk, possibly high, and definitely like he was dreaming.

Patrick huffed out a disbelieving laugh. "Immune? I don't think there's a single person on this planet who's immune to your flirting."

"Then why didn't you ever..." Tobias trailed off, confused, and suddenly a little hurt.

He didn't like when others understood things he didn't. It made him feel like a fool, like the butt of a joke no one had told him about.

Patrick seemed to realize, and he carefully held Tobias's face in his hands, speaking with the softest voice.

"Tobias, you're incredible. You're the life of every room you walk into—a candle in a world of moths, if you want me to be poetic about it. I've wanted you forever, but you were always surrounded by these beautiful people and I didn't think I could compare to that. I... I was just some guy."

"Some guy?! Patrick, you're..." Tobias paused for a moment, wanting to find the right words for all that Patrick meant to him. In the end, it was quite simple. "You're everything. You always have been."

Patrick smiled, and it was the most beautiful thing Tobias had ever seen. He felt his own face mirroring the expression.

"You're beautiful," Patrick told him. "You've got the greatest smile."

Tobias preened. He'd heard the words from others before, but it turned out that none of those times could even *begin* to compare to being on the receiving end of Patrick's praise and admiration.

"Are you sure? I mean, you're not wearing your glasses," he couldn't help but tease.

"Don't need 'em. I've dreamed about that smile for years."

Tobias grinned wickedly. "You've dreamed about my mouth, huh?" he purred, and he felt the shiver of excitement that ran through Patrick in response.

He kissed Patrick's neck and felt the other man swallow. "I've got you," he promised.

Tobias heard Patrick's head thud softly against the pillow as he began trailing kisses along his collarbone and down his chest, tasting the sleep-warmed skin.

The other man let out a surprised moan and cursed as Tobias gently bit down on the skin of his abdomen.

"Fuck... This certainly was not on today's bingo card."

Tobias looked up to give Patrick the most affronted look he could muster. "Bingo? Really? I'm about to blow you and you're thinking about bingo?"

Patrick let out a breathy laugh. "Sorry. Please proceed."

And Tobias did, acting out a fantasy he'd enjoyed time and again, closing his lips around the head of Patrick's hard cock and working his mouth up and down the shaft until the hands desperately clutching his hair were shaking. He was sure he'd completely wiped bingo and every other coherent thought from Patrick's mind.

The broken noises Patrick made as Tobias's tongue beckoned him closer and closer to orgasm would be recorded in his brain forever. And when Patrick's wrecked voice warned him of the end just before bathing Tobias's tongue with warm spurts of himself, Tobias almost came then and there, despite not even touching himself.

Slowly kissing his way back up Patrick's spent body, Tobias was suddenly grabbed by his shoulders and pulled eye-level so that Patrick could slot their mouths together.

"My turn," Patrick mumbled between kisses.

Tobias gasped as Patrick's hand slid down his stomach and beneath the waistband of his pajamas to find him hard and waiting.

Tobias let out another choked-off gasp as Patrick tightened his grip around him. Rolling his hips forward, Tobias effectively trapped Patrick's hand between their bodies for a moment.

"You'll ruin me for anyone else," Tobias panted, not sure if it was a warning or a request.

"Oh, that is *absolutely* the plan," Patrick replied with an uncharacteristically smug grin, swallowing up Tobias's next gasp with another kiss. "I want you," he whispered.

"For how long?" Tobias hated how unsure it sounded, but he couldn't help but ask.

The question made Patrick pull back and he looked at Tobias as if he'd actually heard the world of insecurities in those three words.

"I want *you*, Tobias," he repeated. "For as long as you'll want me."

Looking at Patrick's face, Tobias believed him, and his heart swelled with love.

"I'll want you forever," Tobias vowed, for once not caring whether the words sounded cheesy or cliché. It was the truth.

Patrick grinned, happy and genuine with a hint

of mischief. He winked and leaned in, whispering, "Prove it." ♥

THE CYCLE REPEATS

 by Viola Layne

"We shouldn't be doing this again," I murmur, but I still tilt my head so Wyatt has a better angle to latch his mouth onto the side of my neck. "... especially here, where someone could see us."

He hums his agreement, yet continues sucking at my tender skin. Grabbing my hips, he draws me backward against him, and I smell the familiar whiskey-scented cologne clinging to his skin. I wonder if it's from the bottle I bought him for Christmas or if he's bought a new one since we broke up.

Finally removing his mouth from my neck with a faint pop, the tip of Wyatt's nose brushes against my jaw as he addresses my concern. "You're probably right. But do you *really* want me to stop?"

My assurance that I do dies in my throat as his hand slides up my body, leaving a trail of tingling goosebumps in its wake. When it reaches my breast, he cups it through the silky lime-colored satin of my dress and my heart begins to race. I *bet* he's getting off on feeling the pounding in my chest and knowing he's the cause of it.

Normally, I try to mask my reactions to his teasing, unwilling to give him the satisfaction of seeing how easily he can make me fall apart. Yet as his thumb begins to rub languid circles over one covered nipple—causing it to pebble instantly under his touch—I melt back into him.

"Damn you, Wyatt Sutton," I mutter through gritted teeth, my eyes fluttering as the tingling sensation begins to migrate down my spine and between my legs. Leaning my head back so it rests against his shoulder, I begrudgingly gasp, "No. Don't you *dare* stop."

I swear I can feel that cocky grin of his as he brushes his lips against the curve of my ear. "If you insist."

Suddenly, my world unexpectedly shifts as Wyatt whirls me around to face him. I try to regain my bearings, but before I can, his mouth is devouring mine. Instinctively, I part my lips, allowing his tongue to slip in and tangle with my own. He tastes like bourbon and regret, and I'm hungry for more.

One of his hands finds my breast again as his other grasps the back of my neck. He guides me backward until my shoulders bump into one of the marble pillars on the edge of the room, just out of view of the ballroom doors. I thread my fingers through his dark hair—he's let it grow out since the last time I saw him, the loose strands brushing his sharp cheekbones—and draw him deeper into the kiss. Following my lead, he presses his body against mine, and I suddenly find myself trapped between a rock and a hard place—literally.

I guess he needs this just as badly as I do.

No one has ever made me feel the things Wyatt Sutton has, and I doubt anyone else ever could. It's been four—almost five—months since our latest breakup, yet it feels like we've never been apart. We know every inch of one another, and we fit together like puzzle pieces. It's chemical, sometimes almost spiritual, and neither time nor distance has ever changed that.

However, the physical aspect of our relationship has never been the problem; it's only once we leave the bedroom that the issues start. Incredible sex can make you overlook a lot of things, but eventually, the fighting and tears outweigh the euphoria, and everything inevitably falls apart. Then, months later, we are irrevocably drawn back into each other's orbit, only for the cycle to repeat itself.

Over and over, always doomed to suffer the same tragic fate, never learning from our mistakes.

Yet even though I know this will be the unavoidable outcome, I don't care. This isn't about our past or what happens after tonight. It's about this moment. Beyond that, nothing else matters.

As Wyatt grinds his hips against mine, I feel the throbbing between my legs growing stronger and I need *more*. I try to raise my leg to wrap around his waist. However, my detestable bridesmaid dress hugs my legs too tightly, and the slit only reaches mid-calf, severely restricting my movement.

When my attempts to free myself become more intense, Wyatt pulls back, his brow furrowed and a slight pout on his lips. His eyes sweep across my body, probably trying to understand why my moans of pleasure have suddenly turned to grunts of frustration and if he is somehow the cause of it. When he finally spots the reason for my squirming, he grabs the top of the slit to try to adjust it—though it does little to help.

Throwing up my hands, I grumble, "Just rip it."

He raises an eyebrow. "Are you sure? You don't want it as a reminder of your sister's *special day*?"

I hear the sarcasm he adds to the end of that sentence, but I'm honestly a little touched that he asked. Usually, given the chance, he'll rip my clothes off without a second thought. I've lost a few expensive designer dresses over the years that way.

But I nod, my attention already turning back to his lips, and how to get them pressed against mine once more.

"I've hated this *fucking* thing since the moment Trisha picked it out. Now that her wedding's over, I was planning on burning it the moment I got home. So rip it in half, for all I care."

Something flashes deep within Wyatt's olive eyes. "Don't tempt me, Clover," he growls, but there's a slight tremor in his threat.

This is the first time I've seen his perfect mask of control slip all night. It galvanizes me, and I grin as I lean in close. "Where's the fun in life without a little... *temptation*?" I whisper the last word before lightly nipping at his bottom lip.

He locks eyes with me, and time seems to stop. I can almost taste the desire hanging in the air, thick and heady. It makes my head spin and my knees grow weak as I wait with bated breath for Wyatt to make his next move.

Suddenly, he grabs my dress and rips the slit clear up to my hip. I gasp, my eyes growing wide as they dart around the room looking for anyone who might stumble upon us. It was already going to be hard enough explaining ourselves if we had been caught before, but now that my ass is practically hanging out of my dress, it'll be nearly impossible.

Once I'm satisfied we are still alone, I shove Wyatt in the chest. "What the *fuck?!* I wasn't serious about ripping it that far!"

I try to hold the frayed material together, but he pushes my hands away, leaving my bottom half on full display. "I was."

He slips his fingers beneath the torn fabric and slides his hand over my skin until he's cupping my backside. His lips curl upward as his fingers dig into my bare skin.

"You little minx," he mutters, the sound rumbling deep in his chest. "To think you haven't been wearing anything under here this whole time. Was that for my benefit?"

"You w-wish," I gasp, my breathing growing more ragged with every squeeze of his hand, the heat between my legs building once more. Did I in fact refrain from wearing anything under my dress in the hopes that Wyatt would notice? Absolutely. Though I'd rather die than give him the satisfaction of admitting that to him.

Instead, I tease, "But you know m-me. Always r-ready in case the opportunity *arises*." A sly grin spreads across my face as I roll my hips into his.

The pale green hue of his eyes darkens as he licks his lips. "That's my girl," he purrs, his praise sending another jolt of electricity through my aching core. He groans as he buries his face in my neck. "*God*, I missed this ass."

As his hand continues to knead my cheek, I arch back into his touch. With my legs now freed, I hook one around Wyatt's hip and pull him into me. His leg slips between mine, causing his thigh to brush against my exposed folds. Calmly, methodically, he begins to move his leg in time with his fondling of my ass, and I quiver in his grasp. Already I can feel the familiar pressure growing in my belly, across my lower back, and I grind down harder on his leg.

But then, he slows. His leg still slides against me, but now at a pace that leaves only a slight tingling where before there was a building tidal wave. I squirm against his thigh, silently urging him to pick up his pace, but Wyatt ignores my unspoken pleas.

I should have expected this. Now that he's got me needy and desperate, he's dragging this out just to torment me. My suspicion is confirmed as he raises his head, that familiar self-righteous gleam in his eyes. He believes he's got all the power. However, he's forgotten that I don't give in so easily.

As he continues his leisurely teasing, I slip my arms from around his neck and straighten up, rolling my eyes. "Stop acting so smug and just get on with it. You want this just as much as I do."

Wyatt pauses his movements altogether, one eyebrow cocked. "You think so?"

"I know so." Reaching forward, I grab the prominent bulge in his slacks, squeezing his dick and causing it to jump in my grasp. "Or did you forget that I can *feel* it."

A guilty flush spreads up his neck so I squeeze again just to remind him he isn't the only one with power in this situation.

A stifled groan reverberates in his throat as his dick jerks again. His eyes roll back slightly, his body goes slack against me, and I revel in the fact that I've given him a taste of his own medicine.

Unfortunately, my victory is short-lived. As soon as I remove my hand, Wyatt regains his composure. Running his hand up to push loose strands of hair off his forehead, his smile returns. This one is much more devious than the last and, at that moment, I know I'm in trouble.

"Careful, Clover. Two can play at that game," he taunts, rubbing his hand against the exposed skin of my hip where he tore my dress. Then his fingers slide under the material, skimming across the tender skin at the apex of my thigh before brushing across my soaking slit.

My breath hitches in my throat as a shiver of anticipation dances through my system. But he doesn't leave me waiting long.

Without warning, he plunges two fingers deep inside me.

Collapsing back against the pillar, I gasp as my muscles tense, clamping down on the unexpected— but very welcome—intrusion.

Wyatt doesn't give me a chance to adjust. He

begins moving his fingers within me, stretching my walls and hitting all the places that make my toes curl and hands claw frantically at the sleeves of his suit jacket. A desperate, ragged moan is torn from my lips. Then, as his thumb brushes purposefully against my throbbing clit, the moan becomes a high-pitched squeal.

I buck my hips, urging him to go deeper, to give me more. And he complies, his devilish grin never wavering as he drives me closer and closer to the edge.

Then, just as suddenly as he entered me, Wyatt retracts his fingers and steps back.

The loss is earth-shattering. The pillar is now the only thing keeping me from collapsing in a heap on the ground as my legs tremble beneath me, my greedy folds fluttering for more. I have no idea why he's stopped or what he plans to do next, but I need him to fill the emptiness he's left within me. And soon.

Panting for breath, I watch as Wyatt holds his fingers up to the chandelier, the twinkling lights reflecting off the wetness collected there. Bringing them to his face, he inhales deeply before shifting his eyes back to me.

With a wink, he gloats, "Turns out, I can feel how much *you* want this, too."

When he slides his fingers into his mouth, I

almost come right then and there. The game is over and he has won.

While I have enjoyed our teasing, I'm done playing games. I'm just about to tell him to hurry up and fuck me against this pillar *right now*, when I hear a chorus of laughter drifting from behind the door across from us. Instantly sobered by the sound, all thoughts of continuing evaporate as I'm reminded of where we are.

With trembling arms, I push myself to my feet while simultaneously driving Wyatt away. "We can't do this."

All the haughtiness etched on Wyatt's face instantly shifts, his victory turning to defeat. Looking like a puppy who just had his favorite toy snatched away, he asks, "What's wrong? I thought—"

"No. We can't do this *here*. We need to go somewhere more private," I clarify, placing one hand gently against his cheek. "I'm not going to have the only thing people remember about my sister's wedding be that I fucked my ex outside the reception while they were serving cake. Trisha would never let me live that down."

Wyatt's shoulders relax as his grin returns, though with slightly less confidence than before. Reaching into his back pocket, he pulls out a key card and holds it out between two fingers.

"Well, I just so happen to have the hotel room to

myself tonight since Jackson will be staying with his new bride. Care to join me?"

For a brief moment, my mind flashes to tomorrow morning and the inevitable chaos that will ensue as soon as someone realizes what we got up to. My neck is still throbbing from where Wyatt had been sucking on the sensitive skin, and I can almost feel the hickeys already forming. If the past is any indication, all the concealer in the world won't completely cover where Wyatt has staked his claim on me, and it won't take anyone more than one guess to figure out who put them there.

I'm sure several people—my sister and her new husband included—have placed bets on whether Wyatt and I would fall back into each other's beds tonight. But really, what did they expect would happen when they made us best man and maid of honor at a wedding with an open bar?

I wonder if anyone was stupid enough to bet *against* us.

Plucking the key card from Wyatt's fingers, I purr, "What are we waiting for?"

I grab his tie and drag him toward the elevator doors at the other end of the long hall, my free hand clutching the torn edges of my dress at my thigh. He follows obediently, and I'm slightly surprised he doesn't try to regain control of the situation. Although, the fact he can keep his hands firmly on my ass the entire time may have something to do with it.

Luckily, the area around the elevators is empty, so no one sees us trying to slip away. It's truly a miracle we haven't been caught by now. I can't even imagine what would have happened if one of my parents had stepped out of the ballroom for some air. They never liked Wyatt much anyway, but finding him knuckle-deep in their little girl's pussy would not help rectify those feelings.

It's not until I hear the elevator arriving that it dawns on me that it may not be empty. Panicked and out of time, I shove Wyatt behind one of the voluminous potted plants decorating the area around the elevator doors. Caught off guard by my sudden attack, he stumbles back before clipping his knee on the side of the planter and is sent crashing to the floor.

I hear a grumbled, "What the *fuck*, Clover!" just before the doors to the elevator slide open—and reveal there's no one inside.

Glancing down at Wyatt, I put one finger to my lips and bat my eyelashes.

"*Oops*. Well, better safe than sorry," I grin as I offer him my hand.

He slaps it away and climbs to his feet, a sour scowl carved on his face. Stalking past me into the elevator, he throws himself against the back wall, crossing his arms over his chest while muttering under his breath. I roll my eyes and follow after him.

I press the button for floor forty-six then turn towards him. As the doors slip shut and the elevator begins to rise, I saunter over to Wyatt and place my arms on his shoulders, my fingers sliding into his hair.

His scowl doesn't soften, but he unfolds his arms, placing his large hands on my hips.

Leaning in so my lips almost brush his, I coo, "I'm sorry, baby. Did you hurt yourself? Do you want me to kiss your knee and make it better?" I shimmy my chest against his, trying to brighten his mood.

And it seems to work. Sliding his hands back to cup my ass, a faint grin spreads across his face.

"Sure. And while you're down there, I've got something else you can put your mouth on." He ruts his hips into mine—as if his meaning hadn't been perfectly clear.

Smiling back, I scratch at his scalp with my nails as I whisper in my most sultry tone, "Maybe if you behave until we get to the room. Then I'll wrap my lips around that huge cock of yours and— *Goddammit*!"

All flirtation immediately evaporating, I once again shove him to the side so I can get a better look at my reflection in the mirrors that line the wall.

Less than an hour ago, I was the picture of perfection. I had spent a lot of time and energy making sure not a single hair was out of place for Trisha's big day (and more importantly, her wedding photos). But now I look like I'm on my way to audition for clown college.

My red lipstick is smeared across the lower half of my face, staining my fair skin a faint pink shade that grows darker around my lips. The perfectly crafted updo I paid a lot of good money for has collapsed; half of my auburn hair tumbles loosely around my face while the other half tries desperately to hold some semblance of the once-beautiful style. And despite this brand of mascara claiming to be waterproof, black smudges darken the area under my eyes from the tears of pleasure Wyatt had drawn from me. Last but not least, my ruined dress sways gently around my legs, threatening to flash myself in the mirrors if I'm not careful.

I gently touch my cheek as I sigh, "God, I'm a hot mess."

Seemingly over his little fit, Wyatt wraps his arms around me from behind, drawing me into his chest. Pressing his lips to my temple, he hums, "You're gorgeous."

"No, I'm not." I try to shrug him off but he only hugs me tighter. With a huff, I stop struggling and say, "Besides, that's easy for you to say. You still look like you stepped off the cover of *GQ*."

The few strands of long, dark chestnut hair that have fallen across his face only serve to frame his eyes, making the green hue seem even more intense than usual. His perfectly tailored suit still looks as pristine as ever, despite all of my grinding and grasping at it. And even the sloppy smear of my lipstick across his mouth only serves to enhance the fullness of his lips, which has me subconsciously licking my own.

Damn him.

Wyatt chuckles. "I never said you looked flawless, I said you look *gorgeous*. You spend so much time trying to convince everyone you're perfect and in control, that seeing you like this—knowing *I'm* the only person who can make you come undone— makes me..." he trails off with a deep groan.

I feel his cock twitch against my ass. I start to grind back against him, but Wyatt gently stops me and turns me around, reaching up to toy with a strand of my hair that has tumbled in front of my eyes.

Twirling it around his finger, he murmurs, "So I don't care if anyone saw us leave together, or if they want to make a big deal about this tomorrow. Tonight, you're mine."

There is a tenderness in his touch that hasn't been

78

there before. And while his eyes still burn with insatiable lust, there is something sincere there, too. Just a flicker, a fragile crack in his self-assured facade.

He swallows hard, his Adam's apple bobbing in his throat. Then, as he cups my cheeks in both of his hands, he whispers, "Because you were right, Clover. I need you just as badly as you need me."

He leans forward and presses his lips to mine. The kiss is soft and warm like the glowing embers that remain once the heat of a raging fire has died off. And while I know the flames will burst back to life the moment we get to his room, I embrace this often-unseen side of Wyatt while he's willing to share it.

I've never told him the truth, but I would trade all the sex and mind-blowing pleasure we share to have *this* version of him all the time. The man who makes me feel treasured and adored rather than just an object of his lust. The loving, tender man I've seen behind the shield of arrogance and ego he protects himself with. But he's not able to fully give me that side of him—not now, maybe not ever—so I keep coming back for these fleeting glimpses of the man I love, taking the sex as my consolation prize.

The elevator slows as we approach our floor, and we reluctantly pull ourselves apart. Already

I can see that Wyatt's mask has returned, his full attention now only on one thing. And as much as I love him—and I truly do—part of me wonders if this is really such a good idea. After all, we've tried and failed at this relationship six times before, and I don't think I'm emotionally strong enough to go through it a seventh time.

Yet as the elevator doors open and he takes my hand, I don't say a word. I'm too afraid that if I do, this will end and I'll lose him for good.

And I won't let that happen.

I *need* Wyatt. He's like a drug and I'm an addict taking my first hit after months of sobriety. I know I shouldn't, that this will only end in disaster and pain, but I'm already too far gone. From the moment his lips burned against my skin, this outcome had been inevitable.

So, I remain silent as he leads me towards his room, and I leave the fallout for future Clover to deal with.

God, she's gonna hate me. ♥

THE SOLSTICE BALL

❤ *by Olivia Lockhart*

Lauren

My shoulders tensed each time a person brushed by. It seemed odd that the slinky red dress, bundled safely in its garment bag, weighed so heavy on my arm. Regardless, I didn't want it incurring any damage on the way to the ball.

Relief flooded through me as I stepped inside the first-class train carriage, a smiling member of the crew taking my luggage and hanging the dress safely. Yet as I headed towards my row, familiar frustration bubbled within me. What was the point of reserving seats when some stranger always made themselves at home?

I plonked myself down in 5-A, leaning on the small table that sat between me and my new companion.

"I'm sorry..." How ridiculously British was it to begin with an apology? "... but I reserved that seat for my friend, he'll be here any minute."

The man looked up from his book, his forehead creased a little as if I'd interrupted his concentration. Then, the cutest smile broke out, his lips rising slowly on one side and creating a dimple in his cheek.

"Have I changed that much?" he asked.

I was mortified. "*Jake?!*"

"Did you not recognize me?" His fingers tched against his stubble as he watched me, his eyes roaming over my features.

"What did you do with my best friend's geeky little brother?" I asked, my cheeks burning a little as the train doors swished together and we began our journey.

"You say it as if I was twelve the last time you saw me. I've only been gone two years. I'm thirty now, all grown up."

He certainly was...

When my best friend, Viv, had suggested Jake as a fake date for the company ball, I'd pictured him as he had always been. Sort of apologetic, always in the background, hiding behind floppy hair and baggy T-shirts. But this man...

His toned body was all too apparent under his shirt, his skin tanned, a smattering of freckles I'd never noticed before dancing across the side of his neck. And those eyes... surely, they were new?! Dark and intense, nestled under the longest lashes I'd ever seen. It was mortally unfair for a man to possess such incredible eyelashes.

"Complimentary champagne?" the crew member asked, as she moved amongst the passengers in her crisp uniform.

I was still processing Jake's effect on me as he turned to her and nodded, before passing me a flute of bubbles.

"How was the trip?" I asked, before sipping my drink.

"Incredible. I feel focused, energized. Took me a while to catch up, I guess, but I'm ready to start life." He focused on me with a smile, "And how about you, Ms. Vice President of the company? You're incredible."

"Thank you. I worked like crazy for this. And I really appreciate you keeping me company this weekend."

"Hanging out with you is far from a hardship."

Every summer, the Solstice Ball would be the talk of the company. A glorious, sun-fueled affair to celebrate our successes and reward everyone's hard work. These parties were known for their extravagance, their indulgence, and each year I'd watch as couples lingered in dark corners, stealthily escaping to their rooms, barely allowing the elevator doors to close before their hands and mouths tangled.

I'd invited Jake so I'd look part of a couple, more successful, so I'd fit in somehow—but that didn't explain the excitement fluttering within me as the train whisked us to our destination.

Jake

"You look amazing..." I couldn't keep my eyes off Lauren as we met in the corridor, ready to head to the grand marquee housing the ball.

"Couldn't let Viv's baby brother down, could I?"

My mouth twitched, I wished she'd stop thinking of me as Viv's brother and see me as the man I was now. The man whose teenage crush had grown to so much more.

"Speaking of looking amazing, where did all the muscles come from?" Lauren squeezed my bicep with a cheeky grin.

"Ashtanga Yoga," I said, ripping my thoughts away from how stunning she was in the red dress. "It changed me, not just physically, but mentally, emotionally. I realized I didn't want to be the guy turning thirty, still living like a student, and *still* filling his body full of junk."

"You look like a different person."

"I think I was a late bloomer," I replied.

"What are your plans, now that you're home?"

I told her how I wanted to open a studio as we circled the room, nodding and smiling at people whose names I would never remember. It didn't matter, though. There was only one person I was here for, and right now, she was on my arm.

I took the fake date thing seriously, after all— I wanted it to lead to something real. As Lauren introduced me to her colleagues, I slipped my arm around her waist, unable to stop wondering what her skin would feel like underneath the red silk.

She began to lean into me, and as we talked, I swore her eyes kept falling to my lips. Was she playing along, or could this be something more? I didn't know, but clearly this was my chance to confess, to let her know she was my walking fantasy and I wanted nothing more than to worship her.

"Shall we dance?" I asked, holding out my arm and stepping towards the tiled floor.

"Sure..." she murmured, her gaze intent on mine. I'd never seen her look at me like this, it had to be something. *It had to be.*

I held Lauren close as we swayed to the band. I couldn't quite believe she'd grown even more beautiful. Of course, I'd seen pictures of her on Viv's Instagram while I was away, but a camera couldn't do her justice. And beneath all the beauty, and that body I craved, she held a confidence I hadn't seen before. As if she didn't care what the world thought, she was doing things her way.

"Lauren," I murmured into her ear. "Why so tense? You're dancing with your date, breathe…"

"You're so different from how I remember, that's all. This doesn't feel like dancing with someone's little brother."

Perfect.

"Don't think of me that way, not tonight. You're exactly how I remember. You were always round at ours when I was growing up. And that spotty, teenage, hormonal version of me was very… *inspired* by you."

She gasped, pulling back a little, but I kept hold of her hands and moved her close.

"Jake! Don't be daft. I'm fifteen years older than you."

She felt incredible, and without thinking, my fingers began to play with hers in our interlaced hands.

"I'd get home from college, and you and Viv would be heading out. I used to dream about touching you. If I'd written down all my fantasies, they'd have described *you*. Long legs, that silky chestnut hair, gorgeous green eyes, lips that looked filthy yet pure all at once—"

"Stop it!" she giggled, her face against my neck as we moved to the music.

"At least now you feel relaxed. You don't know what it took for me to admit that. It felt wrong to leave it unspoken."

She'd never know the nerves that had threatened to paralyze me. I don't know how I kept dancing, but now it was said... it was done.

All that was left was to see if she, somehow, felt the same way.

Lauren

"I appreciate you being here tonight, that's enough. You don't have to pretend it's more, Jake."

"Lauren... I'm not pretending." He pulled back, his eyes searching mine.

"Did you never notice? I could barely speak when you were in the room, I'd just blush and mumble and hurry up to my room to think about you."

I bit my lip. "I thought you were having an awkward phase..."

The music snaked around us; slow, dreamlike. He felt incredible and it seemed the most natural thing in the world to lower my head to his shoulder, to rest it there, while his words flowed into my ears.

"Not at all, I simply found you far more intriguing than girls my own age."

"Ah, teenage hormones. I bet you're glad those thoughts are in the past."

"They haven't gone, I've just learned to hide them better." His voice dropped a little as he added in a low murmur, "You've gotten sexier while I was away."

"Stop teasing me," I smiled, my cheeks burning as I stepped away from the dance floor. "I need a drink."

He nodded, his forehead furrowed in contemplation as we walked slowly towards the bar. I ordered two whiskeys, focusing on the splash of amber into the crystal tumblers, as Jake's gaze burned into me.

"There's not going to be a reciprocal moment, is there?" he asked. "Where you tell me you fantasized about me, too."

I noted the raised eyebrow of the barman and snagged the drinks, then headed towards the quieter terrace, motioning for Jake to follow me.

"I think it would have been a tad inappropriate," I began, as the dwindling rays of sun and evening air washed over me. "... given the age gap."

"Maybe then, but not now."

The words seemed to stick to his lips, I couldn't take my eyes off his sharp cupid's bow as he spoke.

I took a steadying breath. Sipped the whiskey. Told the truth. "I might not have been fantasizing about you then, but tonight I can't stop."

His fingers stroked the inside of my wrist, the most delicious sensation. "What are you thinking?"

"That we should go upstairs and make some fantasies come true..."

He leaned in towards me, his lips closing over mine. My hands trembled, and he encased them in his as he kissed me.

His lips were hot, dusted with whiskey and the promise of other places he could put them. The kiss begged for my body, and I was enthralled as he moved to my ear and whispered, "Let's go."

I attempted to look innocent as we made our way back through the crowd, towards the main building. I was giddy with anticipation until a familiar voice boomed out.

"*Lauren!* Lovely to see you. Have you met Jasmine?"

Max, the head honcho. My boss—with the worst timing in the world.

"Max, lovely to see you too. And no, I don't think I've had the pleasure. Nice to meet you."

"You, too," she replied, toasting me with her glass.

Jasmine was a clone of his last five girlfriends, I noted, unsurprised.

"You finally gave in and brought a man?" Max nudged me with his elbow, and I stumbled against Jake, who steadied me with a firm hand. A hand I wanted all over my body right now.

"I'm Jake." He stepped forward with his hand

extended, whilst the other rubbed circles along the base of my spine. He felt good through the silk, but I wanted to be out of this dress.

"Good to meet you. What do you do, Jake?" Max asked as I shuffled around awkwardly, trying to hide my desire.

"I was in software design, but this one," he squeezed my waist tightly, lavishing me with a dazzling smile as his eyes flitted across my chest, "... made me realize I needed to focus more on my inner self. I'm opening a yoga studio."

At this point Jasmine looked up, and I spotted her double take. Her smile widened as she took in all the same things I had—his height, his broad chest, the almost-black hair that curled delicately around the base of his ears. Plus those eyes—they needed a warning label.

"You should combine the software and the yoga, make an app, or get yourself on YouTube. Jasmine is always doing some sort of workout on there," Max suggested.

I coughed and went to step away, but Jake pulled me close, pressing a kiss to the top of my head. Each delicate touch sent more sparks flying within me. I took a deep breath in, allowing his scent to wash over me, imagining it all over me.

Him all over me...

"It's a good idea, I'll keep that in mind," said

Jake.

I slipped my hand inside of his jacket and around his trim waist, adoring the tremble that ran through him as I stroked above his hip.

"Well, I best mingle. Lauren, you're positively glowing, he must be a good influence on you."

"Thank you, Max."

As soon as Max and Jasmine turned away, we hurried back into the hotel. Giggling as we reached the elevator, Jake pulled me to him, his mouth urgent on mine. As the doors opened and we stumbled inside, I wanted nothing more than to tear the suit from his body.

"*Ahem—*"

We broke apart at the realization we weren't alone.

"I'm sorry," I gasped at the bellboy. "Didn't spot you there."

"Apparently not. Floor?" He raised his eyebrow as he looked between us.

"Three, please," I mumbled.

The air was thick and exhilarating. We stood side by side, not speaking, Jake's hand clutching mine.

I clenched my free hand to hold back the trembles of anticipation, anxious to be out and away from the stranger who'd interrupted what had been the most exhilarating kiss of my life. It felt like the slowest elevator in the world.

As we eventually entered my room, the charge between us seemed to slow into something sensual, unhurried.

Jake loosened his tie and threw his jacket over the back of a chair, igniting a pulse inside of my very expensive underwear which hummed with longing for his touch.

"I'm feeling the pressure now," Jake confessed as he sat on the edge of the bed.

"We don't have to... if you don't want to."

"It's not that, I want to. *Fuck*—I've wanted this forever. You're perfect, this feels like a big deal. I never thought I'd speak those words to you. Tonight just felt right."

"I'm nervous, too," I confessed, taking a tiny step closer to him. "But I want this, I want *you*. I'm glad you confided in me. Tell me more."

He let out a long, slow breath as my hand ran up and down his side, lifting his shirt to touch the supple skin beneath.

"I hadn't thought this far ahead."

I drifted my lips across his earlobe. "I have my own fantasies, you know. Bringing a ridiculously hot, younger guy up to my room *definitely* features. Maybe I've dreamed about this."

I grazed the backs of my knuckles across his thighs. "About my legs wrapped around your waist, my nails scraping down your back, hearing what you'd sound like when you're deep inside of me."

Jake groaned, deep and rumbling from his chest. I'd always wanted to elicit that sound from a man.

"What if one night isn't enough?" he panted. "I've wanted you for so long, Lauren."

"Then take me."

My fingers curled around the side of his neck, the skin warm and soft as I pulled him toward my waiting mouth.

Jake tasted incredible—fresh yet familiar, like a night in the rain—as my lips rubbed over his. He kissed me back, tentative for a moment until his mouth opened, urging mine in its wake as the kiss grew in passion.

His fingers moved into my hair, his motions slow and delicate as he touched me with wonder.

I allowed my own to rub across his neck, slipping inside of his collar and loosening it.

"Did it start like this? In your imagination?" I asked, as he scattered kisses along my collarbone.

"My favorite one went a little differently..."

"Tell me," I urged.

"After you and Viv would leave, and I'd seen you all dressed up, I'd disappear up to my room sharpish, because I could never hide how turned on I was." Jake smiled softly at the memory of his fantasy.

"I'd lie in my bed, close my eyes, touch myself,

and imagine that you ran back in because you'd forgotten something. But instead of going into Viv's room, you appeared in mine…"

"What did I do then? In this fantasy."

"You looked surprised for a moment, that gorgeous mouth of yours in a perfect little 'o' as you watched me. I, of course, stopped what I was doing," Jake chuckled. "I was absolutely horrified at being caught. But you closed the door behind you, walked slowly over to me, letting your dress fall to the floor. Then you crawled up onto my bed and started using your mouth…"

Heat flared bright between my legs.

"I think we should make that happen. I'm going to nip outside. Maybe you should relax on the bed, Jake…" I curled his name around on my tongue, before grabbing him for another kiss. His mouth was exquisite. Then I ducked out of the room before I could change my mind.

I couldn't stop grinning. Who knew making unspoken fantasies come true would be this much fun?! I knew I looked flushed, my nipples hard points under the silky dress. I prayed nobody would walk down the corridor as I bounced around, anxious to feel him on me, in me.

I waited two minutes, then let myself back in.

"Sorry, forgot my ba—" I'd planned to let the words tail off in mock shock, but there was nothing false about it.

Jake was an Adonis, and he was on *my* hotel bed. Shirt open, trousers abandoned, those dark eyes trained on mine, his tongue flicking out to lick his lip, and his hand—*fuck me*—his hand... moving up and down, slow and firm, all along the length of him.

This one image was the utter definition of lust, and words deserted me as I drank it in.

I'd never be able to unsee this. I never ever wanted to.

"Yes, Lauren," Jake said quietly. "Your mouth looked exactly like that. *Fuck*, yes..."

His head fell back a little as he sucked in a long breath, his throat catching with desire.

I unzipped my dress, wriggling a little as I walked so it fell to the ground, leaving me in my underwear and heels.

I crawled onto the bed, moving towards him on all fours. His eyes dropped to my chest, and I stopped for a moment to unfasten my bra, dropping it to the floor as my gaze followed his hand... all the way up and down... all the way, each and every time.

I looked up at Jake, his eyes stormy under those dark lashes.

"Don't stop," I begged. "I like it."

His Adam's apple bobbed deeply in his throat as I moved lower, blowing hot breath onto the tip of him, watching in delight as he shivered.

As his hand reached his base, I took him into my mouth, delirious at the tremor in his thighs. I moved up and down in time with his hand, falling in love with the feel of him, the heat, the rigidity, his taste... I wanted to devour him.

After a few moments his hands grasped at my hair, a deep groan falling from his blushed lips as he began to rock into my mouth. I was so turned on, without meaning to, I'd begun to rub myself up and down on his leg, and it felt incredible.

Suddenly Jake stopped me, his hands firm on my shoulders, then cupping my chin as he pulled me up his chest.

"I want you so much I feel like I'm going insane," he murmured, before his tongue was back inside my mouth, and he pulled me flush against his body.

Jake

This *woman*... I'd imagined that fantasy over and over, but the reality had been phenomenal. Mind-blowing.

Lauren, here with me... getting herself off on my thigh as we kissed, frantic and wet. It felt completely animal, out of control, but also entirely natural. I'd hoped we'd have chemistry, but this was off the scale.

"Have you got a condom?" she asked, although it came out more of a moan as my fingers circled her nipples, hardening them to peaks that I couldn't wait to taste.

"In my jacket," I motioned towards the chair I'd thrown it over. I hadn't wanted to tempt fate, but I'd bought a pack on the way to the train station, hoping against hope that luck would be on my side.

I went to stand but Lauren clung to me, her legs tightening around my waist, arms looped around my neck, her mouth continuously seeking me out. It was as sweet as heaven and sexy as hell, and I was desperate to taste every inch of her. Make her mine all night, then wake with those beautiful eyes watching me, as I'd kiss her, tell her how much she meant to me...

I smiled at the thought, and she sunk her teeth playfully into my bottom lip. I slid my hands under her, supporting her as I made my way to the chair. She obviously wasn't getting down, and that was fine by me.

"Good job you did all that yoga, hey?" she teased.

"Not quite sure I can get to the inside pocket without dropping you," I said as I leaned down and reached into the luxurious black of the suit.

"Wall," she motioned behind her.

I took great delight in pressing her up against it. My mouth dropped to her neck, kissing every sensitive spot available. She writhed against me, wanting more, and I sucked in a deep breath of anticipation as my hand slid down her smooth stomach and into the sinful lingerie she wore.

So hot, so fucking *wet*... I almost lost it right there. Nothing had ever been this intense, this passionate. She nuzzled me, whimpering, as I tentatively rubbed a finger inside of her. She groaned deeply, rocked against me, her body urging me for more.

"Where the hell are they?" I mumbled as I tried to reach lower into the jacket, while still supporting Lauren and giving her the pleasure she so deserved.

"They?" she asked as her fingernails trailed lightly up and down the length of me.

"It was a box..." I could barely speak. I adored the urgency with which she wanted me.

"A box? All for me?"

"All for you," I moaned as her fingers circled my tip, causing a deep shudder within me.

"Found them—thank *fuck*..."

To my horror, I fumbled with the foil, all nerves and tension before Lauren took it from me, letting the wrapper fall to the floor.

My eyes locked on hers as I braced her against the wall, and she rolled the condom onto me, slow and steady. Her confidence was such a turn-on. I twitched in anticipation, but there was something I needed to make sure of.

"You sure you want this?" I whispered.

Her pupils dilated, midnight black as I tugged her underwear to the side.

"More than anything. Now, *please*..."

The "please" was still spilling from her lips as I pressed her tight against the wall, and then my body turned to starlight as I entered her. She changed my life at that moment, I swear, as I thrust slowly inside, deeper with each breath.

We paused for a moment, the two of us, gazes locked, breath hot and mingled in front of our faces. Completely one... she was perfect.

"Jake... *fuck*—" Lauren moaned, and I couldn't contain this any longer. My body pounded hers up against the wall, faster, hotter, and needier with each second.

She buried her fingers in my hair as I drove into her, again and again and again. Until my name fell from her lips in breathless gasps, her legs tightened, gripping me inside of her, her body trembled in pleasure. I was lost... lost as she begged me to never stop.

I carried Lauren over to the bed, eager to explore more. She stretched out, languid and soft, post-orgasmic and half-ragged with delirium as she smiled at me. The sexiest look I'd ever had the pleasure to see.

"That was amazing," she murmured, as I ran

kisses up the hot skin of her stomach.

"Who said we were done?" I bit on my bottom lip as I moved back inside of her, suppressing the urge to chase my own release too quickly.

I wanted so much from Lauren, but if this was the only night I got, I wanted to make the most of every second.

"You should have told me sooner..." she gasped, her back arching up to meet me, her hands grasping for me, urging me deeper.

"It just means we have a lot of time to make up for..." I grabbed her ankles and pulled them up onto my shoulders. "You might need to arrange a late check-out, I have a lot of Lauren fantasies to get through."

Her squeal of delight told me that wouldn't be a problem. ♥

SALVAGED

♥ *by Jasmine Luck*

It's been a whole year since I laid eyes—or hands—on Sawyer.

Sometimes, in my darker moments, I get to wondering if I dreamed him up. His lick of dove-gray hair in an otherwise unruly mass of umber. The languid, verbose way he speaks; as if he swallowed a sedative and the dictionary, together, on one wild night.

I can hardly feel the ghost of his touch anymore.

If I ever recalled it properly to begin with.

"One last venture, darlin', and we'll be set for the remainder of our days. I'll be prostrate at your feet with my haul, 'fore you even know I'm gone."

How I clung to those words for the first few weeks. And clung to them still when the communicator crackled now and again, but without a trace of Sawyer's syrup-over-broken glass tones.

I moved doggedly through the days at first. Our

planet makes life easier than for some. Nova III is a pleasant enough home. Clean air, plentiful water. Things any spacer would fight tooth and nail for.

The twenty-foot trees had taken some getting used to, but I now found them a comforting shelter from what I knew to be the merciless expanse of space. Beyond the atmosphere of every planet lay light years of darkness, scattered by a careless throw of pinprick stars.

I know Sawyer exists, somewhere out there, in the endless tunnel of black. I've got the proof; the prints from an ancient Polaroid camera, a lucky find in a junk shop on Utania. The matching roll of film, luckier still, had been sold to me for an obscene price, the shop owner practically salivating as he named it.

Of course, I had paid. Since I'd learned how it worked, pictures of Sawyer have littered the cool unit.

I stare at the squares of paper, cataloging his features again. His slightly crooked smile—one he jokes is a reflection of his skewed m orality. His soulful eyes, the color of liquid drinking chocolate, the luxury Central Space stuff, not the lackluster powder that's served in most spaceports.

I trace my index finger over the dimple in his cheek, the photo paper cool and impersonal under my skin.

"I miss you," I'd whisper to the photos, for the first few months.   Hoping he'd somehow hear. Wherever he was.

Then the weather turned colder, the huge trees changing from purple to a deep gold, the wind dropping.

His side of the bed remained unslept in. After two weeks, I'd finally given in and torn off the sheets, washing them, soaping away his scent.

I cried, the first night my bed smelled of laundry powder and not Sawyer's skin.

And I sobbed unspoken words into his pillow.

I'd held them close to my heart the day he left, lips clamped shut by past heartbreaks. By losing people I'd loved before.

I'll tell him when he gets back.

Stupid.

Words of love, like best clothes and best china, should be used. Not saved, gathering dust behind locked doors.

Too bad I'd learned that lesson after school finished.

Sawyer left a few pieces of clothing behind. I slept in one of his shirts until the hem grew threadbare, unraveling at the same rate as my faith that he'd ever return.

When it totally fell apart, I, ever a make-do-and-mend gal, snipped off the collar and rolled it up,

105

tucking it into a locket he'd given me. I'd chastised him for wasting credits on such fripperies, but he'd only smiled, and cupped my cheek.

"Perhaps it's overstepping the mark, Sunrise, although I'd wager you know that *propriety* and I have never quite seen eye to eye, but I chanced upon this, and thought of you. I am but your humble servant, hoping for a crumb of your affection."

I'd worn that locket ever since.

If not for my work, I probably wouldn't ever have left the walls of home, the only place where if I really concentrate, I can still *feel* Sawyer.

But the Botany Hub keeps me busy. I work with a team, cataloging seeds and herbs and testing their healing properties, assessing their suitability for splicing together as remedies.

Painstaking work, and half the time it's fruitless, but what choice do we have?

Here on the Outer Rim, there's very little Medi-Care equipment, and chances are, if you come across some, its owner met an untimely end just days prior.

My team's friendly. Mostly human, which isn't unusual in the OR, especially because Nova III has breathable air for us.

We all gathered after work last week, in one of the few drinking holes set up here. One of my colleagues invented a cocktail right there on spot—it turned out orange, and he called it sunrise.

Sawyer would've laughed. Winked at me. Settled his hand on my thigh suggestively.

But he wasn't there, so no one touched me.

Fuck, I miss being touched.

The days start to pass in an aimless blur. Nova III's weather is either cold or colder. The chill sinks its teeth into the ground so deep, you're always surprised not to see marks.

The screen in the canteen at the Botany Hub shows a wealthy woman of Central Space preparing for Christmas, decking out her home in rich baubles, while complaining of the uncomfortable weather.

"Rich asshole should try livin' on the OR," a woman on my team grouses in her thick accent, and we all chuckle along. "Her nipples'd freeze off."

After work, I return to my empty home, and stand in front of the cool unit, looking without enthusiasm at the collection of food inside.

As I mentally flip-flop between leftover bread stew and seitan patties, the door buzzer crackles to life.

I cross to it, depressing the button to connect. "Hello?"

It groans to life, static heavy, before a gruff voice demands: "Taitai?"

Must be a lost delivery driver. Although it's been a long while since I ordered food to the door.

And even longer since I gave anyone permission to use that nickname.

"Yes, that's me."

"Sawyer asked me to bring him here," the voice grouses into the comm. Almost like it's an imposition.

I thank The Redeemer that I didn't take anything out of the cool unit. I'd have dropped it clean onto the floor.

"Say—say that again?" I have to force the words out. Surely, I heard wrong.

The person repeats it, adding, "And he's heavy. Can we come up?"

My heart pounds hard, and I press my hand to my throat.

"I'll come down." My whole body trembles as I pocket my access card, hurry down the single flight of stairs, and yank the door open.

The human man, older than me, sporting a chrome left leg that has seen better days, gazes at me steadily.

He's holding up a very bedraggled, heavily stubbled Sawyer. I'd recognize that hair anywhere; that stubborn jawline.

But I can't see his eyes. They're bandaged.

* * *

Sawyer's been a salvage merchant for years, spending his time hopping from one floating shipwreck to the next; turning over objects covered in grime and blood, one at a time, and occasionally finding his palm filled with treasure.

I met him when he staggered up to the back of a long line at a MediCare clinic on Thitune. Lost in my thoughts, and in considerable pain, I'd only noticed him when he fell into me. I turned, catching him in time to stop him hitting the ground face first.

He'd managed to force a strained smile. "Thank you. I'm a lamentable man at present."

I shrugged. "None of us are in great shape; wouldn't be here otherwise."

He tried to stand unaided, and struggled, so I propped him up, looping his arm over my shoulders. In spite of his injured state, and a wide bandage tied around his middle, dark with blood, he smelled of the outdoors; wind-blown and meadowy. A near impossible feat.

"You good?"

He breathed in raggedly. "Thanks to you. But it seems I've lost my manners along with too much blood. I'm Sawyer," he added, wincing.

I eyed the bandage around his body. It had been poorly tended to, no doubt, but like most people, he probably didn't have access to MediCare like a Dermiseal Rod, instead depending on subpar self-administered aid, or clinics like these, run by good-hearted volunteers.

"Li Yingtai."

"Pleasure makin' your acquaintance," he wheezed. It was sort of endearing, but it would have been *more* endearing if he wasn't probably about to pass out from blood loss.

"How did you....?" I gestured to his abdomen.

"Oh, this." He attempted to grin, but failed. "Mis-understandin' between friends. Might've involved a large amount of credits. And yours?"

I awkwardly pushed up the sleeve of my free arm to show him swollen flesh, pinpricked with an angry, spreading rash. "The perils of working in botany—surprise allergies. I actually think it might be infected."

It burned with the rage of a thousand suns.

Sawyer frowned in sympathy. "A fine pair we are. And yet more wretched I'd be, alone, if you hadn't been here."

I shifted to better accommodate his weight. He was warm against me, the heavy stubble on his jaw brushing my forehead. "Anyone would've helped."

"You're wrong 'bout that," he murmured back. "I meet more charlatans than most in my line of work, but overall, people care little for each other. Meetin' you has been like seein' a sunrise after days of darkness."

I scoffed at his ridiculous sentimentality, but inside, something unfurled inside me. A longing I hadn't acknowledged for many years.

We stayed in the queue, me holding him up, him occasionally commenting on others waiting, or feeding me snippets of his life, for another three hours.

By then, I knew I wouldn't be walking away from him.

* * *

Sawyer clears his throat. "Taitai? Is... that you?"

He murmurs something additional, but his voice is low and weak; his words unintelligible. No quick quip, no crooked smile.

No attempt at joviality.

I want to go to him, but I'm frozen. My heart pounds.

"He needs to rest," the man interjects tersely, and his words stir me from inactivity.

Looking past him, I see his vehicle. The glider is in about as good a state as the driver's prosthetic leg.

"Of course. Come—come in." I stumble over the words like a calf taking its first steps. I almost fumble my key card, then use it to call the elevator. As it whirs down the shaft towards us, I finally allow myself to look at Sawyer properly.

"Keep going forward," the driver tells his charge, tone softer now, and I wonder if the man was part of the salvage crew, this go-round.

Sawyer obeys silently.

I ache to touch him.

I'm terrified to touch him.

Is he—can he see?

What if his eyes are gone?

I swallow back a parade of gory possibilities and a rush of bile.

The three of us ride the elevator up to my floor. I'm keenly aware of Sawyer behind me. My stomach dips and flutters with feelings I can't even name.

When we arrive, I busy myself with unlocking the door, and holding it open.

The driver heads for the couch without asking. Finally, my brain kicks into gear and I hurry over to assist him as he lays Sawyer down. That first touch, feeling the warmth of his body against mine, sends a flush of recognition through me, so intense that my eyes burn.

I kneel next to the man I love.

about you."

"I don't think ever he shuts up about anything," I observe, and I receive a more genuine smile in return.

Sawyer shifts on the couch, and I gently smooth my fingers over the silver-gray tuft in his hair. It's just as soft as I remember.

He turns his head towards me. "My... deepest apologies. For the delay."

On hearing his voice—by far the most *integral* part of him—the dam breaks, and I bury my face in the crook of his neck, sobbing, my own voice cracking like dry ground without water for too many days.

"I'll, um, come back later. Gotta, um... yeah," I vaguely register the driver saying, his footsteps getting fainter.

The door bangs shut behind him.

I cry until I'm wrung dry, my hand pressed to Sawyer's chest, just feeling his heart beat sluggishly against my palm.

After a time, Sawyer's arm curls around me. His fingers play in my hair.

"Your hair's still as soft as spun sugar. I remembered you right."

And those words make me cry harder, press myself into him.

"I was beginning to think I dreamed you up. I

thought maybe I'd never see you again."

He huffs, like I should know better, like it hasn't been a full year. "Know that it was ever my most acute intention to return to you."

Taking care to be gentle, I skate the tip of one finger along the edge of his bandage. "What happened here?"

His face twists. "A thoughtless lapse in judgment, for which a high cost was levied."

"Can you—are you allowed to take it off?"

He frowns, pensively. "I'm near certain the specified time has passed." But he hesitates. "You're not guaranteed to like what you see."

I very gently tug at the cloth. "Maybe let *me* be the judge of that."

He stays obediently still as I gently untie the knot affixing the cloth in place, unwinding it.

His eyes are closed, lashes as full and long as ever.

I swallow back a wave of trepidation.

Sawyer opens his eyes.

They're still ringed with the bright copper I remember, but inside that, everything's cloudy. Sort of like the sky after a storm.

"Can you see?" I ask, my voice breaking a little.

"Shapes. Light, sometimes. No real detail." He shuts his eyes briefly, and a tear slides down his cheek. "Only damned thing I want to see is right here, and I'm deprived of even that." He slides a hand along the bed, then up my arm, so he can cup my face.

When his eyes open again, to those cloudy spheres, I'm overcome with a crashing wave of sadness, and a whimper escapes me.

Sawyer misinterprets this and turns his face towards the back of the couch. "I'll understand, should you no longer find me pleasing—"

I turn his face back to me, and cut off his words with a kiss.

There's no reality where I won't want Sawyer. He's a perfect puzzle of a man, with his archaic speech, his bottomless heart, his quick wit.

This is our first kiss after a year of ragged heartache, half an empty bed, endless nights of staring at the sky, willing it to return him to me. Begging the universe to stop hoarding him for itself.

His lips part under mine, and I taste him—cheap black coffee, too much sugar, and it's so strange yet so familiar that I hear myself moan, and without conscious thought, I'm clambering onto the couch and covering his body with mine.

His arms wrap tight around me, and we kiss for moments that stretch. Time ceases to mean anything.

When we eventually part, he whispers, "My fears were selfish, out there. Shuffling off this mortal coil without ever holdin' you again."

I don't know what to say to this. My own fears were of equal selfishness.

Our bodies warm each other. At length, my tears dry up.

"Tell me about the job," I say. "What took you so long?"

Sawyer sighs, not unhappily. "The tale is a long one, involving perilous choices and absent engine parts. I fear at this moment in time, my energies would be best spent elsewhere." He slides his hand down my body, pressing our hips together, and— *oh*.

Everything inside me sits up and begs for his touch.

Anywhere.

Everywhere.

"Don't you need to rest?" I try to do the right thing. He must be beyond exhaustion.

"Not nearly as keenly as I need you. I've *prayed* for this moment. Don't make me wait a heartbeat longer."

His quiet plea breaks me. "Shall we... I mean... the bed?"

His mouth creeps up into that crooked little smile I adore, and *there* he is. There's my Sawyer.

"Too far. Couch is surely wide enough."

It's his smile that galvanizes me into action. I've

never been less graceful than now, as I take my clothes off in a sort of frenzied ballet. Sawyer does the same, somewhat hampered by his injury, and I help him along, too eager to stop and kiss each inch of skin revealed. There'll be time for that later. Later, I'm going to sleep curled around him, press my back to his front and listen to his heart beating until I can't discern its rhythm from my own.

Right now, if he doesn't make love to me, I might die from this desperate, clawing need.

When we're finally, gloriously naked, I crawl over him. I keep my gaze on his. Maybe he can't see me, but I hope he'll be able to feel the connection.

We used to spoon on this couch regularly, for a lazy post-dinner movie, screened on the wall from an old projector Sawyer had salvaged on a job. Sawyer would lay behind me, languidly warm, providing a running commentary because quiet wasn't something he was capable of.

"Please," he whispers now, voice cracking, and I bend to kiss him. His hand caresses my hip, and his touch is the sweetest wildfire.

Our tongues dance as I balance myself on one arm and use the other to wrap my hand around his erectio   feels so warm and solid and *alive* that I have to swallow back the urge to sob with relief. I palm him in long, hard strokes, relishing the way he shudders with pleasure, his head tilted back, eyes closed. My inner muscles clench in anticipation.

Sawyer trails his fingers hesitantly over my belly. "As loathe as I am to admit this, I'm unsure how useful I'll be here, without eyes—"

"Shut up," I bite off the words against his lips. "Just touch me. You *know* me. You know what I like."

I'm already wet, and he curses when he finds me that way. The first tentative circle of his finger and thumb on my clit is bliss. Then his muscle memory kicks in, from years of making love to me, and he applies himself to the rhythm that makes me see stars.

The sharp pleasure of his touch makes me tighten my fist on his swollen flesh.

He drags in a breath. "This is gonna be over before the first act, if—"

I don't let him get that far. I settle his cock between my legs and slide him home.

His eyes roll back in his head, and his free hand clenches my hip hard, holding on. I relish the small hurt. The truth of it. That he's here.

I lean down and capture his mouth in another kiss, and the couch creaks beneath us as I set a punishing pace.

After so long, the stretch is divine. Sawyer's throaty growl tells me he concurs.

"Your cunt has ever been without equal," he rasps

out. "Faultless. Paradisaical, and my own hand never could compare."

"Sawyer, *please*," I groan, feeling my muscles fluttering. "Don't stop touching me."

"I could never deny you anything, Sunshine, even if I wanted to."

The familiar circle of his finger pads over my sensitive flesh is all it takes for my muscles to contract, milking him for all he's worth. The pleasure's got teeth as it chews through me, my whole body shuddering with the force of the orgasm.

Sawyer tumbles over that sweet cliff edge at the same time, biting his bottom lip as he spills inside me, his gaze dark, hot and urgent on mine.

I slide bonelessly on to his chest, inhaling his scent as he pants, shivering with the little aftershocks of amazing sex.

Our breaths fill the silence, until he murmurs, "As I stared the reaper himself in the face, my one thought that was in a lifetime of salvage work, the only thing I ever found worth a damn was you."

* * *

I wake in full panic mode, bolting upright, until I realize that Sawyer sleeps beneath me.

While he slumbers, I settle back down, and study the skin around his damaged eyes. It looks normal.

Hard to believe he's mostly blind, now.

It's true that carving out a life on the Outer Rim takes hard graft, but surely there's a better way forward than going back to salvage.

Besides, surely he won't be able to. The dangers would be untold.

We could eke out a living on my pay. It'd be sparse, but what more do we need than food and each other?

"If those thoughts reach just a few decibels higher, I'll need ear defenders," Sawyer drawls.

I sigh in mock-annoyance. "It's no wonder your crew dumped you back here. Got tired of you running your mouth, I expect."

His lips curve in a slow smile. "I expect."

I sit up, sliding off him. "Wait here."

I cross the small space to what passes as our kitchen, and set to work preparing a reviving herbal drink, one of my more successful Botany Hub experiments.

Guilt spikes as I work; I should have been thinking of his health earlier, and not just sex. Although I'm sure he would say the latter was plenty restorative.

I settle back down on the bed, sitting beside Sawyer. "Drink."

He shifts, sitting up, feeling behind him, and then I gently press the cup into his hands. He drinks deeply, then winces.

I can't help but laugh. He looks as if he's chewed

a swamp-bug. "Maybe I can tweak the recipe and add some sweetener."

"*Now* you tell me." But he drains the cup, anyway.

I set it aside. "Bring that smart mouth to the washroom for a bath."

Once I'm standing, I reach for his hand and lace our fingers together. He stands, too, and I talk him through the steps to the old bathtub, a salvaged item from some years ago. He sits on the edge as I run the water until it steams.

"Is it odd? Not seeing me?"

He considers this. "I can hear you movin' around. It helps."

I shut the tap off and move to kneel before him, settling my hands on his thighs to communicate my intention.

I look at him for moments that stretch, drinking in every little detail. Old scars and new ones.

He strokes his way up my arm, over my shoulder, and cups my cheek. "Don't expect you—"

Sawyer sighs as I map them with my fingers and then my lips, deliberately skating around his erection for far longer than necessary, until his hands tangle in my hair and he moans my name, his voice an octave lower with need.

Only then do I take him in my mouth, re-learning the shape of him with my tongue, getting acquainted again with where to lick so his breath hitches, the exact place to stroke behind his balls to make his cock swell. When I glance up at him, his head is tilted back, mouth slack with pleasure.

A view I thought I'd never savor again.

He cups my cheek, rubbing his thumb over my bottom lip. A warning. "I'm close."

I squeeze his thigh. I want everything he has to give. And a moment later, I get my wish. He tastes of how I imagine the seas of Earth did before humans fled it—salty, sharp, addictive.

I let him linger in the afterglow for a moment before I stand.

"Let's get into the tub."

I assist him, then settle in with my back to his chest, luxuriating in the way his lean body takes up space. Our home has felt so empty, this last year.

His hands skate up my arms and find the nape of my neck. His fingers graze the chain of the locket that hangs between my breasts. "You kept it."

"It was a way to feel close to you."

He washes my hair, slow and gentle. I lean into it, wishing I could somehow capture the feel of his touch, find a way to relive it at my whim.

When his head's lolling forwards, his lips grazing my neck. I flip the seal of the bathtub open with my foot, and encourage him out. He's weak as a kitten, his damp hair curling madly at the edges.

We dry ourselves off, Sawyer's movements somewhat clumsy, and I walk him back to bed before curling up around him.

"No more salvage," I whisper into his shoulder.

"No more salvage," he agrees. "Cedrix—the driver—should be 'round with my share of the haul from this job. It's not all I hoped for, not with the sprawl of crew we ended up needin', but it'll keep us goin' a pretty good while."

He turns in my embrace, presses his lips to my forehead. "I stared into this cavernous steel trunk of riches, beyond what I ever could have imagined. And as they coruscated up at me, all I could think was that I'd toss it all through an airlock, watch them tumble into that endless stygian void, just to get back to you."

I settle my hand over his heart, and the words I'd foolishly kept to myself before he left bubble to the surface. "I love you, Sawyer. Then, now, always."

He salvaged himself from the black spiral of space, for me. To get back to me.

As far as I'm concerned, he's the most valuable item in it.

We drift into sleep. ♥

BRIEF ENCOUNTERS

♥ *by Sabine Marlize*

The evidence is laid out across the room, enhanced by the moonlight seeping from the open balcony window, shining like a spotlight on her indiscretion: her heels by the door, her silk dress thrown carelessly over the chair, his shirt at the foot of the bed, the aquamarine-and-diamond behemoth squatting on the nightstand instead of its usual place on her ring finger...

Mia drafts a reply in her head: *Morning, babe. Met some girlfriends, had to catch up for a bit. Otw home. Safe flight.*

She hates herself for it. Only the most despicable person would come up with an excuse for their spouse while still lying in bed with someone else. Someone whose birthday party was where she'd first met Alexander, her husband. The same someone she's still coming back to after all these years. That very someone who frantically undressed her on the same boat Alex named after her just last month, all with him just an earshot away.

It's over, Mia knows she should tell him. *I'll stay.*

But she's not sure she could hold herself to that.

Year 1

Mia fidgets with the zipper of her pink velvet Moncler jacket, watching the group that's eagerly waiting for the ski lift by the patio.

The four-day event is a grand affair: an all-expenses-paid vow renewal ceremony in Norway for her best friend Vanessa and her husband, Richard. They'd eloped five years ago and never had the time to plan for a proper wedding celebration until now. Limitless food and the promise of an aurora borealis sighting are enough to make Mia tolerate the sub-zero temperature.

She lets out a shuddering cold breath, counting the minutes until the server comes back with her hot chocolate, when a man hovers over her. Theo.

"You're not coming, Mia?" he asks, nodding towards Vanessa and her friends chatting excitedly and taking pictures near the group of reindeer. Theo is a longtime friend of Richard's and a famed photographer to high society and Hollywood stars— and by all measures a very, very attractive man. Honey-colored hair tousled from the wind, piercing eyes somewhere between blue and green, and a killer grin worthy of a magazine cover. And also, the sort of man who usually wouldn't look at her twice.

"Not my thing. I'm just here for the spa and après-ski," Mia answers truthfully, flipping her long auburn hair out of her face. A minor sledding accident when she was seven was enough to make her swear off snow sports altogether—forget about trying a new one.

"Alright, suit yourself," Theo shrugs before flashing her a smirk that makes her stomach flip. "See you around."

As if she had anywhere else to be.

* * *

Later that evening, Mia watches with bemusement as hundreds of Vanessa and Richard's guests dance and drink the evening away under Baccarat chandeliers and crystal icicles hanging from the roof. The renewal ceremony and the accompanying reception are on a level of lavishness unlike anything Mia has ever seen. She smiles when she catches Richard hoisting Vanessa in the air in the middle of the madding crowd, her swirly, sparkling dress casting tiny glints of light around the ballroom.

Mia glances away, running a hand down her

velvet dress to smooth it and debating whether to sneak out, or wait for the happy couple's crowd to wane to say her good night.

"You look bored," a familiar voice behind her says. She turns around and finds Theo approaching her, his suit jacket unbuttoned and a fur coat draped over his arm. His usually wavy hair is slicked back, the ends curling around his ears, the style conjuring a 40s film star in her mind.

"May I?" He points to the seat next to Mia, and she nods.

They sit together in silence, watching the party move around them, with Theo occasionally waving to acquaintances he spots across the room. The tension is almost unbearable. After a few unsure glances towards her, Theo finally breaks the ice.

"So, what's up?" He throws her a playful but curious smile. "Vanessa doesn't throw boring *anything* and no one just sits around alone at a wedding unless they're heartbroken, or... socially inept."

Mia returns his smile with a rueful one. She is neither, simply suffering a pang of loneliness from seeing her friend so happy with 'the one' while she always goes to weddings and get-togethers alone. But she doesn't know this man well enough to say that, nor does she want to make this conversation a pity party.

"It's been a long four days," Mia settles on a simple answer. "I'm just a little tired."

Theo chuckles. "Tired? You barely did anything this weekend."

Mia raises an eyebrow in jest. "If you must know, I've got a deadline waiting for me back home. I'm anxious."

"I guess that's an acceptable excuse. What do you do?"

"I read manuscripts and summarize them for my boss. What she likes gets published, and we haven't had a hit in a year, so I guess I'm just feeling the pressure lately."

"You love doing it?"

"It's just what I do," Mia says simply. "Don't love it, don't hate it."

"Hmm. What would you rather do?"

Mia cocks her head and smiles. "Well, I wanted to be a singer growing up. It didn't go anywhere, so I went back to college, and now I do this." There's no bitterness or regret in her voice, it's just a matter of fact. "What about you? Vanessa told me what you do. You love it?"

"Hell, yeah. I actually started by taking stock photos, some of them ended up as book covers. Maybe you've seen them."

"Maybe. I'd have to look at them to know."

"I'll text them to you. Give me your number."

Theo winks, the grin on his face blooming with cheekiness, and he's already pulled out his phone.

Oh, that's smooth, Mia chuckles to herself. She gave him an opening without even meaning to.

Year 2

Theo groans with release as he nuzzles against Mia's neck, his warmth seeping into her. He drapes an arm over her naked body after she flips him over to catch her breath, gently caressing her skin, his lips against her temple.

He wants her, more than he's wanted anyone in a long time. He's lucky that he happens to be shooting in San Francisco, where Mia had just settled in for a new job in marketing. After a year of casually talking on social media since Norway, it was nice to see each other and catch up in person again. What followed next was simply satisfying their urges—four times including this morning, to be exact.

His hand continues roaming her perfect body and she melts into him, soft sighs nearly tipping him into raring to go again. But he really needs to go.

"My flight's in two hours," he murmurs into her hair, messy from their lovemaking.

"Reschedule," Mia demands, her hand sliding lower to what she wants from him most, driving him mad with want. Theo swallows hard, his eyes darkening as he weighs his options.

"I can't..." he rasps, his voice thick with longing.

"But you want to," she presses, her voice sultry, coaxing him to stay.

He does. *God*, how he does. Every fiber of his being wants to stay, to lose himself in her for just a little longer. But his next project is calling, pulling him thousands of miles away.

"I'd stay the weekend if I could, gorgeous," he murmurs, hating himself for the words. "But I'll see you again soon?"

Year 5

The canals of Venice shimmer in the moonlight, casting a romantic glow over the city.

Mia loved her first visit here many years ago; the museums, the beautiful palazzo hotels, the glide of gondolas at night, the Bellinis at Cipriani's, the music streaming out of Caffè Florian, the walk through flooded water up to her calves across Piazza San Marco.

She would've loved to be back here under different circumstances. Richard's second wedding brings Mia and Theo here, the two finding each other immediately upon entering the venue. Theo even switched out someone's place card for his just so they would be seated together.

"Vanessa would've hated this," he had quipped as a greeting.

It feels a little traitorous being here, even though she thinks Vanessa would've loved seeing her ex-husband find happiness again after her passing. Mia still vividly remembers where she was and what her homemade pumpkin spiced latte smelled like when she got the call from Richard a year ago.

She thought of all the times Vanessa could've restrained herself and stayed home as she should have, instead of going out so often during a pandemic. It was a miracle that Richard made a full recovery after two months in the hospital, but Vanessa checked in and never left. Mia didn't even get to go to her burial. She was left by the girl she'd known since they were both seven years old without a proper goodbye. With Vanessa gone, Mia has never felt so alone.

But Theo is right—Vanessa *would* have hated this. The wedding is too simple for her tastes, lacking her flair for the grandiose. But she would've loved that her ex's new wife is practically her clone: similar frame, waist-length platinum blonde hair, striking gray eyes, and an unbridled joy she radiates whenever she enters a room. Sometimes Mia gets a glimpse of Isabella from behind and half-expects to see Vanessa's face when she turns around.

Swallowing a lump in her throat, Mia squeezes Theo's hand for comfort and he brings it up to his mouth to kiss it, his eyes meeting hers to silently say he gets it. He knows what she's feeling. He was the first one to reach out to her after Richard broke the news of Vanessa's death, five months after their encounter in San Francisco. Since then, a brief tryst here, a little rendezvous there—all to help each other feel a little less lonely, and it always works. She doesn't expect anything different tonight.

* * *

Seven weeks pass without hearing back from Theo since she left him hot and spent in his suite at the Danieli, and a text arrives one afternoon inviting her to his 33rd birthday party in Palm Springs the following weekend. He's only a little older than her, she learns now. She doesn't know why she never bothered to ask his birthday, and she realizes that he's never asked hers, either.

The party is at a film producer's mid-century modern mansion sheltered by looming palm trees and canyons, whom Theo met while photographing guests at Oscar parties. The vibe is surprisingly intimate given the extensive guest list of people from all walks of life, all equally as successful (or more) than the host: athletes, movie stars, Grammy winners, heirs, authors whose works Mia used to pass along to her former boss... and a certain tall, dark, and handsome Alexander Mateo, whose mother founded one of the biggest recording labels in the world.

"Alejandro," he corrects Theo's introduction for him, extending a hand for Mia to shake, a brilliant smile plastered on his face. "Alexander is just better for business."

Year 6

Something's up. She can feel it. For the past few weeks, Alex has been occupied with something he's not sharing with her. Hushed phone calls in the middle of the night. Last-minute trips to wherever for what he said were meetings. Canceling date nights mere hours before.

Even now, he's busy fiddling on his phone and hasn't even complimented her yet, and she's changed outfits three times today. She hates to assume the worst, but... Vanessa had warned her all those years ago about getting involved with powerful men, long before she found a good one in Richard.

"You'll always come second to their work," she'd said. "And they always have someone, some*ones*, on the side. So don't get too attached."

Before she can indulge in those jaded thoughts, she and Alex arrive at his mansion in Sausalito that he bought only a couple of months ago to be closer to her. The past year of being with Alex since he offered to fly her back on his jet from Theo's party has been a joyful bliss. He's more than she could ever ask for, a perfect package of a gentleman: kind, loving, patient, incredibly smart, and wealthy on top of it all.

She'd never dated older before—eleven years to be exact—but she's pleasantly surprised by how well they fit. They found out they shared the same interests and values in life despite the gap, and—Mia thought a little vainly—they looked good together. What started out as a once-a-week date night quickly turned to Alex working from home at Mia's small apartment for most of the week and then to buying a house that she now spends half her time decorating.

"It needs your feminine touch and exquisite taste," he said. "And you'll be living here full-time anyway."

The other half of her time is spent recording for Alex's artists. Mia supposes she could call herself a musician now, as inorganic as her newfound job came about. It beats her previous one at the literary marketing agency and she's grateful Alex's position allowed her to leave that behind. She still doesn't have "it" to be a singer, Alex's producers gently told her, but she plays the piano beautifully and sounds great on background vocals, and she could just do that if she wants to.

"You don't mind going up first, do you?" Alex hesitantly asks, snapping her out of memory lane.

"Everything okay?" Mia furrows her eyebrows. She already knows he'll say he has to get on a business call again.

"Yeah. Just need a little fresh air, is all."

He looks visibly nervous but she doesn't press him. "I could join you...?"

"I'll be upstairs in no time." Alex nudges her with a wink. "Wait for me in bed, will you? Wear the red lace thing you got last week."

Mia's body surges with excitement as she walks through the house, but that doesn't last long when a text shows up from Theo while she waits. She hasn't heard from him in months, relying on updates from Alex when he would run into him at industry events in Los Angeles.

"Don't say yes. I'll be in San Francisco next week, don't say yes yet," it says. She stares at it in confusion before getting distracted by Alex entering their shared bedroom.

An hour later, after they make love, Alex finally pops the question.

"Yes!" Mia screams, without a second thought.

Year 9

She regrets to say that she's the one who started it; the sneaking around, the dirty texts safe in her secret second phone, the excuses, the flights that aren't on Alex's credit cards or his company jet. It's not an unhappy marriage—far from it, to be frank.

Mia wants to say that domestic bliss gets boring but she would be deemed ungrateful for thinking it. She has the perfect husband, perfect marriage, perfect house—or so everyone tells her all the time. But it lacks thrill. They'd ticked off everything on their bucket list that first year, and now Alex is lightly pushing her towards having kids as he's getting older.

She's not against it *per se*, but she's not quite ready for it. She could use a couple more years of freedom from that kind of responsibility, and she thinks Alex would perfectly understand that, but these days she just feels as if she's idly living out a pre-written script of her life.

It's strange to feel caged like this. Mia was never one to seek out "thrills" before she settled down. She had longed for the comfort that Alex is now providing her; there is almost nothing left for her to want. He keeps her well-fed, well-pampered, well-fucked... it makes her want to cry in frustration that she cannot pinpoint what's *wrong* with them. There is nothing to fix because nothing is broken—and yet, it's incomplete. She is happy, she tells herself. She should be.

But as happy as Mia is supposed to be, there is no other high that beats being under Theo, feeling him move inside her, hearing him call her filthy names, letting him put her in positions she doesn't do with Alex. This is what's been missing—though it's no fault of Alex's—desperation for Theo, who now knows her body best.

It had started at Richard's fourth wedding, to another Vanessa clone. Theo admitted that he had wanted her the night of his birthday and for forever, that he regretted he didn't act fast enough, that he had foolishly introduced her to his friend. He explained the pleas he sent over text that night, right after Alex happily called him to let him know he's proposing, and to thank him for introducing you. His absence from their wedding which at the time he said was due to work, but he purposely took a job overseas on the date because he couldn't stand to bear witness to it.

She was too drunk to make the right decision, she wanted to tell herself, and had missed Theo so much that she needed to have him one last time as closure. Just once, she told herself, and then they both would move on with their lives.

Once turned to a second time when one night

Alex brought him over for dinner, and they made use of his car's backseat before he left while Alex was preparing for bed. Again when Theo flew out to Vegas where Mia was attending a friend's bachelorette party weekend. Fourth, fifth, sixth... countless times of seeking each other out whenever possible.

Mia's guilt ferments more inside her each time, and doubles every time Alex remarks that she looks sick (she feels like it) and that he hopes it means she's pregnant. As if she's given access to a reset button, all of that is quickly forgotten with every encounter with Theo.

Year 11

They were bound to make a misstep, it was an inevitability. They were too comfortable in their affairs, too used to Alex never suspecting anything in the two years they'd been carrying on behind his back.

With the toss of a white gold Patek watch onto her lap that both Mia and Alex know doesn't belong to him, he confronts her.

"Just tell me," he begs, exasperated. "How long? What am I doing wrong?"

Nothing, she wants to say. *Absolutely nothing. It's me. We never should've gotten together, it should've been me and him from the start.*

The watch had been on the nightstand on Alex's side of the bed, on the yacht that he had bought for their fifth anniversary. Theo must have forgotten it in his haste to leave, and she had forgotten to hide it along with his jacket that she shoved into her underwear drawer.

"At least tell me who it is," Alex pleads. "Tell me, and I'll forgive you. All you have to do is end it, and we'll move and start over, we'll—we'll go to counseling... Please, baby."

Mia sits in silence. She doesn't deserve him, she knows this for a fact. The right thing to do is to come clean and leave him, let him find happiness again and be happy with someone who'd love him more than she was capable of, who'd give him children without thinking twice.

But she wants it both ways. She wants the security Alex offers, but she craves the excitement that Theo brings her.

* * *

"I know it's him. I know it's Theo," Alex confronts her over breakfast one morning in their newly purchased L.A. mansion. It doesn't feel like a home for her, despite her touches, but now the house feels much colder. Suffocating. "Don't deny it. Unless you wanna tell me my employees risked their jobs to lie to my face."

He sets his fork down on his plate, a touch too firmly. "You've disrespected me, disrespected this marriage, but unfortunately, *my darling*, I do still feel love for you.

"Here's what you'll do. Meet him in public, no fucking funny business. But it's over. It has to be over, Mia. If you choose to stay in this marriage and build us a family, I'll let it go. If you choose him..." Alex gets up from his chair, pointing his finger at her like she's a petulant child. "I'll leave you with nothing. I'll ruin your life."

* * *

They stumble into his hotel room close to midnight, limbs tangling so frantically that it's hard to tell when one ends and the other begins. He looks at her, the soft moonlight outlining her figure, a pang of regret mixing with longing.

Theo had dreaded this moment—he knew it couldn't last forever. What they've been doing has been on borrowed time, time that has now run out due to Alex's legal threat over their livelihoods. He couldn't even ask her to leave him if he wanted to. He had fumbled his chance all those times he didn't stay with her when he wanted to, when he didn't visit her enough in favor of work, and worst of all—when he let her out of his sight long enough for Alex to sweep her off her feet.

He kisses her with fervor, pouring into it all the love, heartache, and desperation he feels for her, hoping she can feel it too. Too much unsaid. Too much time wasted.

Their clothes fall away slowly, piece by piece, his new gold and green Vacheron watch carefully placed on the nightstand next to her aquamarine and diamond wedding ring. He takes his time, his hands exploring her curves, memorizing every detail, every inch of her skin, as if he could hold onto this moment by touch alone.

They fall into a tangle of limbs on the bed; Theo on his back, Mia draped over him with her mouth wrapped around his cock, her knees bracketing his shoulders.

"Fuck, baby. Don't stop, don't *ever* fucking stop," Theo pants underneath her, his hands grabbing and squeezing her ass.

Mia takes him further into her mouth, covering what she can't swallow with her hand, tongue working on him in urgency, needing him to spill down her throat. Two in the morning and they're not even close to being done, wanting their last night together to never end.

Theo's fingers run down the seam of her pussy,

stroking her opening and spreading her wetness before he enters her with two fingers. Tight and soft as ever. Mia moans around his cock and he involuntarily thrusts up, making her gag. He'll miss her.

"I'll miss you," he whispers, when she hovers over him to guide him inside.

Mia gasps with pleasure when she lowers herself down, and she feels her heart pang over his admission. He pulls her down and buries his face in her neck, inhaling her scent, trying to bottle it in his memory. Her arms wrap around his shoulders, holding onto him as she works on his lap, needing him closer. Wanting him to blend into her.

Theo feels his peak getting closer and flips her over. Now he can see her face more clearly; flushed, in ecstasy, but on the verge of tears. He drives into her harder than he's ever done before, needing to leave an imprint inside her, needing her to feel him whenever she's with Alex from now on, needing her to wish it was him instead. Her wanton moans grow louder at the force of his thrusts, and when Mia comes, she does so with a broken cry and rolls over before Theo can see a tear fall.

He peppers her shoulders with kisses, calming her down, assuring her that it's alright. She doesn't say anything, and so neither does he. There are no words that can capture what they've shared all these years, the feelings they kept inside, right when they're about to lose it all. Instead, he just holds her, feeling the warmth of her skin against his, knowing that this is the last time he'll ever feel it.

"Stay," he sleepily whispers as she drifts off to sleep, spent from their lovemaking and her crying.

* * *

Before dawn breaks, Mia is gone. No last words, no goodbye kiss, no *I'll miss you too*, no casually planning for their next encounter. Theo feels the finality of it settle over him like a dark shroud, and he lies in the darkness thinking back over the last eleven years of his life. He closes his eyes, trying to hold on to every single second they shared last night, every movement, every sound, every facial expression.

Tomorrow, he tells himself, will be the start of forgetting.

Year 14

Theo is greeted by a package set on his foyer table after another day of shooting wannabe-models on the beaches of Bali. It's pedestrian compared to his previous job, but he needed the escape, and his nomadic life bouncing around Asia for the past couple of years has been serving him well.

News of Mia's pregnancy mere months after their last encounter sent him running to the soonest departing flight he could get out of the country, and he hasn't looked back since. Not that there was anything to come back to anyway, with Alex making sure he'd never work in town again.

He's been unofficially exiled.

Theo studies the box in front of him; no return address, an expedited overnight shipping label. It's *heavy*, heavier than it should be for its small size.

He frowns. He'd tried his best to make his current whereabouts unknown, even to old friends back home. He runs his thumb over the cardboard seam before letting curiosity get the best of him.

Inside is the long-forgotten Patek watch he thought he'd lost. Still pristine, and by the looks of it, recently cleaned. It sits on a wax-sealed envelope, and he opens it to find a notecard—its letterhead a simple *MM* in blood red.

Theo's heart leaps into his throat.

Two lines of her elegant, sloping script mark the page: an address in San Francisco and a date, seven months from now. ♥

I'D LIE

♥ *by Cate Page*

The first time Olivia saw him was in the pick-up line for Creekside Elementary, her blonde hair piled into a messy bun, mascara smudged across her cheek, the straw from her iced coffee hanging from her lips. She had been arguing with the podcast she was listening to, forgetting momentarily that a school parking lot was probably not the best place to have a one-sided conversation with a C-list celebrity from a decade old reality show.

He sat in a green truck directly behind her, the brim of his baseball cap tilted enough to show off a bemused grin, a teasing twinkle shining in the corner of his eye. Who knew how long he'd been watching, but as far as Olivia was concerned any amount of time was too much.

She remembered the exact moment he caught her eye, white hot embarrassment shooting up her neck, flushing her face bright red, and she muttered a curse up to the sky as she tried and failed not to stare. Even with an entire car length between them, it was impossible to ignore how handsome he was— a nice smile and broad shoulders, one large hand draped easily over the steering wheel.

One half of her mind scrambled, wondering if it was physically possible to sink down into floor boards of her sedan, the other half far too fixated on how beautiful the stranger was.

She didn't have long to worry about it as, mercifully, one of the teachers waved her forward, a sea of second graders pouring out of the double doors at the front of the school. Rosie, of course, led the pack.

* * *

Olivia wouldn't see the stranger again for two weeks, this time as she sprinted barefoot through the school parking lot, Rosie's lunch in one hand, her heels in another. Out of the corner of her eye, she glimpsed him walking hand in hand with his own little girl towards the front of the school, amusement coloring his features.

"That's Rosie's mommy! She forgets stuff a lot," the little girl observed, in that loud way kids do.

Olivia had to remind herself that at that moment it was inappropriate to yell at other people's kids. Of course, it was equally inappropriate to ogle another parent's broad shoulders or the way his T-shirt stretched across those shoulders, but she never claimed to be that *perfect* of a person.

The third time she saw him she finally got a name. He found her in the school gym, a 'Fall Festival' banner hanging above the bleachers, a tray of hastily frosted cupcakes spread out on the table between them.

"These look... interesting," a warm voice met her ears, and *oh—shit*—he looked even *better* up close. Hazel-kissed eyes watched her closely, plush pink lips twisted into a smile, his signature hat tucked into his back pocket, giving Olivia an up-close look at the dark brown curls he had been hiding underneath.

"My mommy made them," Rosie proclaimed a little too loudly, pigtails bouncing in time with her words.

Olivia grimaced at her daughter. "Thanks for throwing me under the bus, kiddo."

She turned back to the man, embarrassed laughter bubbling out of her. "I'm not much of a baker."

"Same," he admitted, one large hand rubbing the back of his neck. "I ended up just donating some chairs I made for the silent auction. Seemed easier."

Olivia's gaze drifted to the display of items up for auction, two beautiful Adirondack chairs, hand-made and stained a rich toffee-brown. She had scribbled a pitiful $50 on the bidding sheet only minutes earlier, knowing full-well she wouldn't be bringing those chairs home.

"You *made* those?"

The man shrugged as if embarrassed, the button-up he was wearing somehow straining tighter than that infernal t-shirt. "It felt a little like cheating since I do stuff like that all day. I work in construction."

"You're not exactly making me feel better. I'm a bank teller. What am I going to offer?"

He laughed again, the creases around his eyes growing deeper. "I mean, I don't think anyone would say no to a big bag of money."

"Fair."

"Mommy, are you gonna make Abby's dad buy something or not?"

"Rosie! Manners, please," Olivia reminded her daughter. She was gearing up an apology when the man chuckled, fished a dollar bill out of his wallet and offered it over.

"Sure. I'll take one."

Rosie's smile was smug as she carefully placed the money in the little cash box the school had provided while Olivia tried to pick the least pathetic cupcake to give to...

"Can I get the name of our first official customer,

or should I keep calling you 'Abby's dad'?"

"James Reynolds," he smiled, licking bright orange frosting from his thumb. "Pleased to meet ya."

"Olivia Meyers."

A sort-of friendship grew from there. Friendly smiles traded when they ended up in the car line front to back. Waves across the pumpkin patch on the class field trip. A quick hello and even quicker goodbye as she picked up Rosie early for a dentist appointment, James there on a similar mission for Abby's yearly physical. Sitting side by side at the same tiny table, watching the girls decorate gingerbread men. Small talk that slowly turned into lengthy conversations, that morphed into inside jokes.

And with each encounter, Olivia's heart beat that much faster, her mouth dry and her cheeks flushed.

It was too cliché. Wasn't it?

The single mom falling for the single dad. Expected and ridiculous, in a way that made Olivia roll her eyes.

It hardly helped matters when she took her crippling confidence into consideration; a kind man raising a daughter all on his own would hardly want anything to do with the messy baggage that sat at her feet. And she had no intention of pulling at that painful thread any more than she needed to.

Olivia made a home in her denial, finding it more comfortable to refuse the truth than dare repeat it. She lied again and again, willing the flutter in her stomach to disappear. It was practiced and perfect, and if challenged, she'd say it with confidence. If anyone were to ask how she felt about James Reynolds, she'd lie.

Not that he made it easy.

With his dimpled cheeks and sweet smiles. The way he held the door open for her, or said hello to her *and* Rosie. How he had locked eyes with her as he licked that awful blue frosting from his thumb.

Six months into the school year (and five months into Olivia's big lie) Rosie jumped into the car waving a neon green flier around, her words stuttering and stumbling over one another. It took a few minutes, but eventually Olivia deciphered the source of her daughter's excitement. A slumber party in the school seemed like a great time for the kids and a terrible time for any adults who volunteered, but Olivia wasn't going to point that out. Not when she had the opportunity for her first night alone in months.

* * *

Two weeks later she dropped Rosie off at the front of the school, her sleeping bag under one arm and her book bag hanging off the other. She gave a wave before sprinting off, screaming Abby's name as if they hadn't just seen each other a few hours earlier. It was then that Olivia noticed a familiar green truck idling behind her, James giving her that same sweet smile that turned her insides to mush.

She waved, letting her eyes linger on the dimple pressed into his cheek, before putting her car into drive and pulling away from the curb slowly, refusing to look in the rearview mirror as she went.

Olivia wished she had planned something elaborate or wild or spontaneous for her Friday night. Her sister had tried suggesting a few things—a club or a bar—Carly always was the more adventurous of the two. She had only laughed, not bothering to remind her younger sister that while she lived in the bustling streets of New York City, Olivia made her home across the George Washington Bridge in the suburbs of Jersey.

Carefully, she pulled her car into a parking spot towards the front of the grocery, a mental checklist already forming in her mind: *wine, frozen pizza, ice cream.*

Olivia couldn't be bothered to be ashamed of her stereotypical choices, too elated at the prospect of a pizza with more on it than 'just cheese' and an ice cream flavor that wasn't named something like "Rainbow Unicorn Sprinkle Explosion." She was trying to decide between Death by Dark Chocolate and Triple Chunk Chocolate Chip Cookie Dough when a familiar voice called for her attention, a warm, wide shoulder pressing into her own.

"I see we're on similar missions."

James was still facing the freezers, but Olivia could see the smile dancing on his lips, his eyes cheating to the side to look her up and down. He held a plastic green basket in his hand, a six-pack of beer and a three-meat pizza placed neatly side by side, an almost perfect match to Olivia's box of rosé and a supreme.

"'The single parent's starter pack' is the official name, I think."

Olivia immediately regretted the words as soon as they came out of her mouth. It wasn't exactly a secret that they were the only single parents in the second grade class. The other parents were shit at keeping their mouths shut, so even if she hadn't noticed that James was always the one pulling dropoff and pick up duty, or the absence of a ring on a specific finger, she still would have found out sooner or later. But what Olivia didn't know was the circumstances, or if James carried the same sense of humor when it came to his lot in life.

The decisive sound of his chuckle chased her fears away. "Think maybe we could package them? Do some clever branding and make a quick buck?"

"*Mmm*, sounds like a lot of work," she replied, clicking her tongue against the back of her teeth.

"Yeah," James agreed, turning to face her. "I say we keep it our little secret."

That same flutter of butterflies erupted inside her chest, warmth spreading across her cheeks, James's gaze holding her steady. The moment felt far too intimate for the frozen food section in the local grocery store, and Olivia started chanting that same mantra inside her head.

The same lie.

He motioned to Olivia's basket, "I won't admit how many times Abby and I had that *exact* pizza after her mom left."

A pink tinge colored his cheeks as he pulled at the brim of his baseball hat. "I was a bit of a mess in the kitchen for a few months."

"Abby seems well-nourished," Olivia pointed out, turning around to lean against the freezers, tilting her chin to look James in the eye. He barked out a laugh, his head falling back with the sound, the column of his neck stretching from the effort.

"Thank fucking god I got my shit together. Especially with her mom on the west coast now."

"Oh, wow... that's..."

"Far? Yeah, but not like I could stop her or anything. Abby goes out there in the summertime and Lucy comes to visit around Christmas. We make it work. Only took a fucking divorce to get us to work together."

Olivia nodded, though having a partner—even one she wasn't romantically linked to—wasn't something she could relate to. She told James just as much right there between the ice cream and the frozen peas.

"Rosie's dad was gone before I could even get the full sentence out. He didn't seem interested, and I didn't have any desire to force it on him."

James didn't say anything but she didn't miss the way his eyes went dark, the fingers wrapped around the handle of his basket flexing into a fist, his jaw ticking left then right.

Far too intimate for the frozen food aisle.

"So, what else is on your agenda for the night?" she asked, the edge of his expression softening at her question.

"Pizza, maybe a movie, and..." his voice trailed off as he leaned in closer. Olivia swallowed around nothing, her heartbeat picking up speed, his cheek brushing hers as he reached down to tug at the freezer door, a blast of cold air hitting her legs, doing little to cool the heat creeping up her neck.

When he pulled back she swore he turned his head just enough for his lips to graze her ear, but before she could register the sensation, James was speaking again, holding up his prize at eye level.

"... some ice cream."

Despite the rapid flutter of her heartbeat, she felt a teasing smile twist her lips. "Butter Pecan?"

"Oh, and what flavor do you prefer?"

She tilted her chin an inch higher in challenge. "Guess."

James rolled back onto his heels, eyes tracing her figure from top to bottom and back. Olivia felt another wave of heat wash over her when his gaze seemed to linger, just barely, on her lips. Eventually he smiled, leaning back in, this time reaching above her head and coming back with the exact tub of Death by Dark Chocolate she had been considering. Olivia held up her basket and he gave her a wink before placing it gently between her wine and her pizza.

The conversation stayed the course while they moved in tandem, shoulders brushing gently as they moved slowly away from the ice cream. They discussed the homework load for second graders, bemoaned late library fees for books they swore never entered their homes, and praised the patience of elementary school teachers. By the time Olivia and James reached self-checkout, they had left the topic of school behind and had moved on to their movie choices for the night.

"I feel like I should do something rated R since Abby isn't home, but honestly I might just try to turn on a basketball game and zone out. What about you?"

"I keep telling my friends I've watched *Bridgerton*, but the truth is I haven't gotten around to it yet," Olivia admitted. "I'm running out of ways to lie about it."

They checked out quickly and quietly, coming back together at the store's exit. James fiddled with the brim of his hat, eyes drifting to the parking lot, but not moving. Olivia was perfectly matched in energy, shuffling from one foot to the other, reluctant to let the moment pass.

Just as she had worked up the energy to say goodbye, James was turning to her, that same smile she had come to know returning in full force.

"Want some company tonight?"

"I... really?"

"Really," he replied warmly.

They ended up back at her place, James's truck following closely behind.

Olivia spent the entire ride—all ten minutes of it—berating herself. James was just being nice. He was nice. He smiled at everyone, he donated hand-made chairs to a school fundraiser. He volunteered to chaperone field trips.

So it stood to reason when he saw the messy mom (the one who forgot her daughter's lunch and argued out loud with podcasts and spilled her iced coffee) alone in the grocery store, he offered to spend time with her.

"He's just being nice."

The words felt half hollow inside her car, the sound of the engine cooling just beneath Olivia's voice. She glanced up, catching his eyes in the rearview mirror, his head tilting to the side in silent patience. She took one steadying breath before flashing a quick smile, her nerves far from calm, and opened her car door. James matched her actions, the keys to his truck jingling as he moved in behind her, his breath warm on the back of her neck.

"It's not much," she shrugged, leading him through the front door and into the kitchen.

He hummed, his steps a beat behind. "Looks perfect to me."

Olivia immediately busied herself with preheating the oven, while James took charge of getting both tubs of ice cream into the freezer before asking her where she kept the glasses. She pointed him in the right direction, then watched quietly as he broke open the box of wine and poured her a glass before twisting the top off one of his beers.

"So... Bridgerton?"

This made Olivia laugh. Loudly.

"You don't want to watch that."

"I don't," James admitted, leaning back against

the counter, one arm braced back to support his weight. He seemed at ease standing in her kitchen, hazel eyes tracing her form from top to bottom.

Olivia tried not to squirm beneath his gaze and failed miserably, suddenly aware that she was still dressed in her work clothes, her blouse beyond wrinkled, and her pencil skirt twisted up around her thighs and exposing the run in her stockings. She considered tugging the offending fabric down to cover the rip, but James had just spotted it, his lips parting around a silent 'oh.'

And before she could stop herself, Olivia asked, "Why are you being so nice to me?"

James seemed to falter at her question, his head tilting to the side again, his eyes searching hers, the words coming to him slowly but surely.

"Liv..." he said quietly, the nickname falling from his lips like it was always meant to be there. "Do you really not know?"

She shook her head, wide eyed and unblinking, terrified if she looked away for even a second he would disappear, the entire evening the cruelest of dreams. James stepped closer, each step measured to the beat of her heart.

"I probably should have been more clear," he whispered, still taking slow steps in her direction.

"Here's your chance."

A smile spread sweetly across his lips at her quip.

"I'm really bad at small talk."

Okay.

"And I think pumpkin patches are really boring."

Wait.

"And I *hate* cupcakes."

Olivia shook her head again, still feeling like she was two steps behind him. "I don't understand."

James stood directly in front of her now, close enough for Olivia to feel the warm flutter of his breath, the mingled scents of cedar and peppermint overwhelming her senses.

"I do those things because I love my daughter, and I would decorate a thousand stale gingerbread cookies to make her smile. But, Olivia, I've never been more excited to chaperone a field trip or break my back sitting in a tiny-ass chair, knowing you'd be sitting next to me."

"James..."

"What I'm saying is," he kept going, his voice starting to shake with intent, "... you make everything better, and I would really like to kiss you."

Something wonderful bloomed inside Olivia's heart, all of the moments shared between them— big and small, long and short—running through her mind. It turned out there had been no need for her lies, her denial only hiding what was, in retrospect, so clear.

It only took a nod and he was leaning in, capturing

her lips in a searing kiss, the palm of his hand curving around the shape of her cheek. Olivia sunk into the kiss, pulling him closer, the butterflies finding freedom in the press of his lips. James gave as easily as she took, parting her lips with the sweep of his tongue, stealing the smallest taste before pulling away, a shuddering breath shaking out of him.

"A gentleman would suggest we eat first," he whispered, the tip of his nose tracing her cheek.

"Good thing I'm not a gentleman," she joked, her teasing laugh stolen by another searing kiss.

What came next was a bit clumsy, shaking fingers and breathless gasps broken up between stumbling steps. They landed on the couch, half-dressed, small confessions and begging whispers kissed into bare skin.

James was practiced in all his impatience, filling her up whole, first with calloused fingers, and then with his tongue, wicked and sweet as he drank his fill. Olivia came hard and fast, her hands buried in his thick brown curls, her back bending up and away.

He took his time after that, stripping the rest of their clothes away, the tremors in his fingertips gone, the hold of his hand steady. Her palm found his heart, grounding herself in the beat of it, even as she drowned in the liquid heat of his dark eyes.

There was one more kiss, then another, some-thing like a promise passed between them, before he sunk into her tight heat, bright white blurring her vision to black.

One, two, three beats of his heart passed before James finally moved, chasing the pleasure that had encapsulated them both.

Olivia clung to him, head buried in the curve of his neck, lips broken around her pleas for more. He held just as tight, lips pressed into a tender kiss to her sweat-slick temple, promising to give her as much as she needed.

She came first, arms and legs wrapped around him, tense and tight and much too much. James wasn't far behind, his hips hammering hard enough to bruise, his touch still so very gentle.

It wouldn't be until a few hours later, one pizza gone and the second in the oven, a box of wine split between them, that Olivia admitted to her little white lie, the words mumbled into James' bare shoulder.

"Are you telling me," he started, pulling her over to straddle his waist, the length of him already hard where it pressed against her, "... that we could have been doing this months ago?"

"You could say that," she teased, pushing her hips down and delighting in the gasp he released.

"Then it's agreed," James said, leaning in to steal

a kiss. "No more lies."

Olivia stole a kiss of her own, the tip of her thumb tracing the edge of his dimple.

No more lies. ♥

WHISPERS OF THE SAND

❤ *by Quinn Perry*

They each dream of brown eyes. Windows of varying shades of umber, of russet, of cinnamon and coffee— the doors to yearning hearts.

Over the years, their love took many forms. The soft whine of a young child pining for affection. The soul-crushing limerence born in a preteen. The feigned disinterest of a teenager. The curiosity of a young adult, carried into adulthood to its rightful place, returning to its earliest form: pure, burning connection. Soulmates.

Five-year-old Aurora carried James in her heart for twenty years, burying him deeper and deeper as each day passed.

And James—well, he never stopped looking for her. Not until, at last, he found her.

* * *

Rain pelted against the windows, staining the parking lot's pavement. A man stepped inside the dive bar, shaking the water from his shaggy, black hair.

Despite the soft ding of the bell overhead, Aurora remained standing behind the bar, her head down, focused intently on the task at hand: scribbling in her notebook, straight lines and sinuous curves that would eventually be carved into clay and stone.

She loved to mold, to sculpt, to create, and build the shapes that called to her. It consumed her, just as much as her desire for him had. It wasn't until the wet, bedraggled man made his way to the bar and pulled out a stool, the scraping sound of wood on wood echoing off the walls, that she looked up at him.

Those dreams of brown eyes ceased the moment their gazes met—they'd become reality for the first time in twenty years.

Her eyes were as fiery as he remembered, set under a pinched brow. But what solidified his conviction was the necklace she wore. A simple gold chain with a seashell, blue and white like the waves. He remembers the moment he found it, the immediate urge to give it to her. She'd kept it safe after all these years.

"*You,*" he wanted to say. But more than that, he wanted to climb over the bar top, scoop her into his arms, and never let her go. He became acutely aware of every single one of his breaths, the entire world thrown into sharp focus, now that he had finally found her. It had taken a lengthy search of dipping and out of coffee shops, bars and taverns, hoping that she was still around after all these years.

He'd gotten lucky tonight, just like he had the day that he met her.

James gazed at Aurora, letting his eyes trace each curl of her hair, the details of her features. She was as captivating as the day he'd met her—no, even *more* so now. And she'd grown, matured, her hips wider, curved, and soft. He sucked in a breath, shifting uncomfortably in his seat.

Aurora frowned, tilting her head at him. "Hello?" she prompted.

His head jerked, gaze meeting hers once more as he stood up straight. "Hmm?" he hummed.

"Anybody in there?"

James's brows raised for a moment, and then he nodded, processing her words. Some of his own sat on the tip of his tongue, boyish and excited.

"*It's me*," he wanted to say. "*It's me, I found you. My girl, I'm your boy. I found you. It's James.*"

But James wasn't boyish anymore. Whatever light, whatever appeal he'd had—despite his violently protective tendencies toward her—was gone. His father had won, had snuffed out any joy, any tenderness inside him when he decided to move away. James had no reason to keep the version of himself he was on the beach alive, not when he wasn't sure he'd see her again. Not when had to survive his father's wrath by fostering his own.

He ran a hand through his hair, attempting to soothe himself. He needed a cigarette, but he wasn't ready to leave her just yet.

Aurora stared, stared until she *knew* him. Who else could it be, walking into her bar on an otherwise uneventful night? Why couldn't he have come sooner? Why did things happen this way, suddenly and out of the blue?

She had dreamed of him, longed for him, begged God and the universe, ancestors and spirits alike to bring him back to her... and here he was. But he didn't recognize her, she assumed by the emptiness in his eyes—

"A drink?" she asked, striving to remain aloof. Her heart pounded in her ears, the rush of blood drowning out anything that wasn't him.

James blinked. She was not the girl he'd met at the beach all those years ago, not in the figurative sense. But he could see her, some glimpse of her in those searing brown eyes. Maybe that meant there was some version of himself from all those years ago still inside him. Maybe there was hope.

He sat, tossing two twenties on the bar top. "Whiskey. A double. Neat."

Aurora didn't move, other than to raise an eyebrow.

"Please," he added, the corners of his mouth quivered as he fought the grin threatening to spread across his face.

Her pour was steady, practiced. James watched her hands, the same hands he remembered diligently shaping and molding sand into soaring structures on the beach all those years ago.

As she pushed the glass across the counter, James murmured a husky "*Thanks,*" one that skated right up Aurora's spine. She ducked her head, spying a bin of glasses at the far end of the bar that needed polishing, something she could pretend she had to do in order to avoid looking at him.

He sipped slowly, allowing the whiskey to warm his mouth before it burned through to his heart. His eyes flickered to Aurora, her curls bouncing, lips moving as if she were whispering to herself as she worked. Too soon, the contents of his glass began to wane, along with his confidence.

He should leave, he knew—go and never come back. He was sure that he would do nothing but complicate her life, imprint on her the mark he's left on everyone he meets, let alone those he gets to know more intimately.

No, James bolstered himself. He couldn't let fear rule him, not here. There was so much of his life under fear's control—he couldn't lose her again.

With one last glance at his empty glass, he stood, walking the few steps to the other end of the bar where her head was still bent in concentration.

"Another?" she asked, keeping her eyes down, staring at the glass in her hand as she wiped it again and again.

When James leaned closer, propping his elbow on the bar, he could smell her perfume, fresh and salty like the ocean. He wondered briefly if her skin would taste much the same before he jerked his head, clearing his thoughts.

"No—thank you," James tacked on quickly. "It was good to see you."

Aurora's eyes snapped up to meet his. She sounded almost offended by his statement.

"*What?*"

James' heartbeat quickened, but he repeated himself, his voice softer. "It was good to see you. After so long."

Aurora's eyes fluttered as the meaning of his words washed over her. He knew it was her. He *remembered* her.

"You, too," Aurora whispered, breathless. Her gaze met his, and she allowed herself to sink into the warmth of his coffee-deep eyes.

James's mouth twitched like he was fighting a grimace—but there was a warmth in his eyes that couldn't be denied.

"You got a pen?" he asked, miming writing with his fingers in the cup of his palm.

"Mmmh," she hummed around the knot in her throat.

The pen exchanged hands, their fingers brushing. In that fleeting moment, James wondered how *so much* longing could be stored in such a brief, innocent touch. He felt winded, all the air leaving his body, and he was suddenly grateful to be leaning against the bar.

Aurora was quiet as James scribbled his number on a napkin, her thoughts racing. He slid it across the bar to her, and Aurora fought the urge to grasp his hand, instead pinning the napkin with one finger. He nodded, raising two fingers in a salute and she nodded back to him, her hair bouncing.

She liked that about him—the few words, the sincerity that bled through his actions. She watched him leave before looking down at the napkin, signed 'J'. At that moment she realized that despite all the years of knowing him, she didn't remember his name.

Children are so silly, so forgetful. It would have been impossible for them *not* to have exchanged names that fateful summer. At one point she must have known his name, and over the years it had faded away, making room for more important information; though as she racked her brain she couldn't think of anything that felt more important than remembering every crumb of detail she knew about him. But the memories of him protecting her and her sandcastles, the way he made her feel important back then, *worthy*, seemed almost engraved into her DNA.

In true Aurora fashion, she didn't say who she was, didn't clarify a thing when she texted him later that night.

* * *

Two days. It took all of two days for them to draw each other in. It started with hundreds of texts shot back and forth, and it ended with one—short, and to the point.

I want you to kiss me.

James had told Aurora that she had to *ask* for what she wanted. That she couldn't beat around the bush or play it safe if they were to be what they'd been to each other so long ago. She had to tell him explicitly that she *wanted* him. There was a part of him that expected her to blow off his request, but her reply had come in quickly.

James continued to stare at it, repeating the words in his head.

I want you to kiss me.

He wanted to kiss her too, he needed it. He was

made for it. Before he could think clearly, he was pulling on jeans and grabbing his keys.

* * *

James's texts ceased for the night after Aurora sent the message, after she'd done just as he asked. The tight coil of anxiety in her chest turned further in upon itself and nestled even deeper. She'd been too forward, messed up everything before it could even truly start. Aurora told herself that was to be expected, she shouldn't be *surprised* that she had fucked everything up.

But it hurt to admit to herself that with *him*, she thought things would be different. How had she messed up something that felt inevitable, that felt as if it were rightfully hers?

Maybe it wasn't, Aurora scolded herself. She tried to keep busy, find anything to do that would dig out the pain, but it was no use... until there came a knock on her door.

Could it be? No, she thought. Aurora cautiously made her way to the front door and peeked through the peephole, slapping a hand over her mouth to stifle her gasp of disbelief.

"You're... *here?*" she asked as she opened the door, looking to James like a curly-haired angel, surrounded by the delicate glow of the porch light.

"I—I wanted to see you," James said carefully, his palms slick.

But it was more than that, he could admit. He *needed* to see her. Even with their history, could he say that? Say that it felt like his lips were on fire at the idea of not kissing her? That his heart dropped into his belly and turned to ash at the thought of leaving her needs unsatisfied?

Something inside Aurora softened, even as she teased, "Our date is tomorrow."

"I can always leave, pretty girl," James murmured smoothly, taking a slow step back.

She reached for him in sync, locking her fingers with his. "Don't you fucking *dare*. Give it to me."

James's mouth twitched. He leaned in, his mouth a hair's breadth from hers and whispered, "Say 'please'."

She felt like a bee stuck in honey. Like his words had cemented her in place and lit a fire deep within her bones. "*Please.*"

"Good girl," he praised, bumping her nose with his own.

With shaky hands, James cupped her jaw, pulling her flush against him. Their lips met with a spark–the same current from a couple of nights ago when their fingers had brushed ever so briefly.

Aurora felt like she was drowning, happily drowning in waves and waves of his affection. But despite the overwhelm, she felt held. She felt safe, like she was exactly where she was meant to be, doing exactly what she was meant to be doing. Abruptly, like a lightning strike, she realized that she loved him.

That monumental notion shattered her feelings of safety, and her breath hitched, her feet guiding her away from him. Away from the thing she had wanted all her life.

James let her go, his brow knitted in concern, though he stayed in place. He didn't want to scare her.

"Aurora?" he breathed softly.

"*Hmm?*" she hummed, her eyes trained on his feet.

James reached out slowly, like she was a skittish animal whose trust was on the line. He caressed her cheek, guiding her gaze to his. "I've got you."

She blinked, letting his words skate over her skin before they sunk deeper. His gaze shone with sincerity. In that moment, it no longer mattered to Aurora that she had never loved anyone before him. It didn't matter if he didn't love her back. It only mattered that they had finally, *finally*, made it back to each other.

The fear swirling inside her burned off and turned to wispy smoke as she lunged for James, guiding his mouth to hers once more.

They tumbled into her apartment, stumbling and knocking into things, a tornado of hands and mouths and *desire*. Every few seconds they were stalled by their greed, pinning each other against the wall, or a piece of furniture; any surface they came into contact with, for leverage against their passion-blinded movement.

"James," she breathed, pulling back slightly to look him in the eye.

His name on her tongue was sugared honey, saccharine and delicious. James was compelled to pillage her mouth with his own, consume all of her sweetness, just to feel the rush of her in his blood. He could see the need there, blazing in her eyes, could recognize it as if it were his own.

"I know, pretty girl," he cooed, running his thumb over the swell of her bottom lip. "Take me to bed."

Aurora kissed at the tip of his finger as it skimmed across her lip, pulling a shudder from James. She grinned, taking his hand and guiding him through the hall to her bedroom where she shut the door.

The air felt charged as James closed the gap between them. His hands fell to the hem of her tank top, letting the pads of his fingers brush against her soft skin before he stilled completely.

"You trust me?"

"Yeah," she murmured confidently, resting her

hands over his. "Touch me."

James grinned, and though she hadn't seen him in years she could tell that his smiles were few and far between. She didn't take that for granted, storing the vision of his delight away in a secret place, proof that *she* had made him happy.

The rushed cadence at which they were moving before didn't resume. Neither of them wanted to miss a single detail, or allow this moment to slip away too quickly. With reverence and patience, layer by layer they bared themselves to one another.

"You're fucking beautiful," he whispered, his voice infused with wonder as his hands explored every inch of her.

"You're one to talk," she quipped, arching into his touch. His hands on her were waves against the shore, knowing where to push and pull, to crash and surround her.

Snorting softly at her wit, James coaxed Aurora to lay back on the bed. For several moments all he could do was adore her, appreciating the way moonlight shone through the window and danced across her skin. He took his place at the edge of her bed, running his hands gently up her calves and thighs.

"Let me get my mouth on you—*please*," he added when he saw mischief flash in her eyes.

James's tongue moved as deftly as his hands,

drawing pleasure from between her legs. The taste of her was heady in his mouth, and he felt he'd never be satisfied. He would live and die here, pleasuring her, loving Aurora in any way she would let him.

"J-James," she stuttered, a hand knotting tightly in his hair as she felt her peak approaching.

"You can take it, pretty girl," he encouraged softly, focusing his efforts on her most sensitive spot. Her legs tightened around his head and he grinned. "Almost there, aren't you? Cum for me, honey."

Aurora felt weightless, breathless. His words, his touch, his *mouth* had her floating effortlessly into her orgasm.

James murmured matter-of-factly, impressing into her his only wish, "I need to have you."

"*Have* me, I'm yours," she said easily, guiding him on top of her.

He buried himself inside her with slow, syrupy movements, and all at once they were taking in the same breath, thinking the same thoughts, feeling the same feelings.

James had never imagined that he could feel so close to someone, not even her, not even with the way she'd been imprinted in his heart all these years. He was distinctly separate, uniquely broken in a way that he never thought would fit with anyone. But Aurora welcomed him with openness, her body taking him as if their coupling was written in stone.

Her love for him sat on the tip of her tongue. As she writhed against him, worshiped his skin with her mouth, sunk her fingers into his silky hair, it taunted her, and Aurora lost her grip on the words as her pleasure began mounting again.

James could sense her drifting away, her eyes going hazy. He slipped a hand in her hair, gathering her closer, reminding her where she was. "Look at me. It's me, Aurora. We're together now."

With a soft breath, Aurora let everything go but him. Her fear and worry, her past and future. She gazed into his eyes—eyes she'd been preoccupied with since she was five years old. She couldn't waste this, not when it could be everything. Her hands gripped his even tighter, her hips moving against him with purpose.

"*Fuck*, James. More, please."

James murmured softly, teasing her with a mock scold. "*Patience*, baby."

"Do I seem like a girl with patience?" she retorted breathlessly, pulling gently at his dark locks.

"You'll learn some for me, won't you?" he crooned, slowing down even more, stretching her until she could take no more of him. Her answer to him was lost as he grinded into her, pressing at the softest spot inside of her over and over until she grew dizzy.

"Gonna cum for me again? I can feel how wet you are."

Aurora knew then that she could never be anyone else's. Her body *knew* him, so much so that as he murmured to her, teased her, she fell over the edge again. Her pleasure spiraled and spiraled, sending her up, up, up, soft cries spilling from her mouth.

Everything went dark for James as she clenched around him, his breath hitching in his chest at how tight she was.

"That's it, honey," he choked out, scratching at the linen beneath them as he rode out his high. "That's it, my good girl. My *perfect* fucking girl."

James bent to kiss her, sealing their lovemaking and all of his praise with his lips pressed against hers. He pulled him with her as he rolled over, enjoying the weight of her body on top of his. She was soft and delicate in his hands, warm and pliant.

"James?" Her voice was barely audible.

"*Hmm?*"

"Was it—did you..."

"Was it what, pretty girl?"

"Good?"

"So good. You're such a *good* fucking girl, pretty baby. C'mere..." He gathered her closer, brushing kisses over her curls. "Was it good for you?"

"Mmmh," she hummed, feeling uncharacteristically shy.

"Good. Do you want me to sleep here?" he asked quietly, pressing the most tender kiss to her temple, hoping against hope that she'd say yes.

She answered with a non-answer, "Only if you want to."

"I do. I'll stay," he said simply.

But Aurora got the feeling he didn't mean it so simply. That his declaration to stay encompassed days and weeks and *years*.

* * *

Sometimes, years before he found her again, James would wake in a cold sweat and reach for her. In the dark, whispers and tendrils of those who hurt him, of those who took him away from her would envelop him as he shed the fog of sleep. He *needed* her and her sunshine to bring him back to Earth.

On those nights, he would stare out the window until the sun came up, snuffing out the darkness. Then he would dress and find peace in the sand under his toes—the sand they'd once played in together.

But when James woke on that fateful night, the night that made him finally feel whole again, his reach wasn't in vain. He sprung upright, his arm searching the bed until his fingers met with smooth, warm skin.

She was finally here.

At the feeling of his urgent touch her eyes opened, immediately realizing his distress. Aurora sat up, slipping her hand into his. "What is it, sugar? What's wrong?"

James couldn't find the words—he never could.

He opened his mouth, trying to tell her everything, but it felt like his throat was closing in on itself. Instead of words, a low whine escaped as he shook his head.

"Okay, c'mere," she whispered, guiding his face into the crook of her neck.

James clung to her, anchoring himself like she was a lone rock in a tumultuous tide.

Despite his silence, Aurora could feel his warm tears falling, following gravity as they skated across her skin. She wasn't sure what to do, wasn't sure how to comfort him—or anyone for that matter. But she would try. For *him,* she would always try to be more.

She thought about the love she shared with her late grandmother, about the love she'd held for James in her heart all those years. Acting on that... it could be enough, couldn't it?

"I've got you." She murmured his own words from earlier in the night back to him, and James melted further into her hold.

Chirping cicadas and the soft creak of the bed

frame as she rocked him grounded James. His breath began to slow and became smoother, and when Aurora felt him relax even further, she guided them both down to lay on the mattress again.

Something washed over her as they laid together, a calmness that felt final. Unmovable. It allowed her to drift off before she meant to, before she could watch James fall asleep, ensure he was alright.

As her gentle snores began, James smiled sleepily, pulling her closer.

"I love you," he whispered to the woman in his arms, as precious as the moon. It echoed to the sands he could see from her window. To the moment they'd first met. To the moment they returned to each other, and to every moment in between that had led him back to her.

"I love you." ❤

ALL OF ME

♥ *by Carmilla Sloane*

Rays of sunlight brightened the sky as the sun peeked out from behind the mountains, casting colorful beams across the lake. Being up *this* early on vacation wasn't Angeline's plan, but the sunrises were too magical to miss. All of her senses were heightened as she basked in her surroundings.

Soon, memories of the last time she was here came rushing back.

It had been a perfect spring day, the sun high in the sky as a breeze danced off the water. Angeline hummed a tune as Gabriel planted kisses along her thigh. Her fingers danced across his arm, stroking imaginary piano keys.

"*Mmm*, I like that," he whispered against her skin.

Angeline smiled, her eyes closed. "Should we write something together?"

"We could…" Gabriel brushed his fingers across

the bare skin between the hem of her shirt and the waistband of her shorts, "... but there's something else I'd enjoy more right now."

Angeline grabbed his hand, playfully biting his fingers. "Everyone's inside."

"We'll just have to be quiet," Gabriel whispered as he stroked the soft skin below her belly button.

The crunch of gravel under tires yanked Angeline out of the memory. Sitting up, she grabbed the sides of the hammock, trying to see around the house. As far as she knew, everyone was accounted for, all five of them.

"I'd know those legs from anywhere." She heard his voice first. A moment later, Gabriel approached, a seductive smile glued to his lips.

Gabriel's husky voice flowed over her like honey. She cursed under her breath in disbelief. As she pulled her legs back into the hammock, his gaze burned into her.

"And *I'd* know the sound of that old-ass truck from anywhere," she snapped back.

Gabriel chuckled at her comment as he moved closer. He took his time, his eyes traveling the length of her. As far as he was concerned, Angeline looked good in anything she wore, but there was something about the band tee and shorts combo that made him feral.

Gabriel lingered, waiting for Angeline to make

eye contact. When she didn't, his gaze drifted to her feet. She was wearing a purple shade of nail polish that used to drive him mad. Gabriel brushed a finger across her foot.

The butterflies in Angeline's stomach fluttered wildly at his touch. Attempting to hide her reaction, she angled her legs away from him.

Gabriel grinned, "Remember the last time we—"

"No one mentioned you were coming," she cut him off.

Gabriel removed his hat, holding it against his chest. "It's called a surprise, sweetheart."

"You don't get to call me that anymore." Angeline finally looked at him head-on, which proved to be a mistake. As much as she told herself to look away, she couldn't. His sapphire eyes held her captive.

Not only did Gabriel sound good, he *looked* good, all five feet and eleven inches of him, packaged up in a strong, lean build with broad shoulders. Angeline noted to herself that he'd gained some weight in all the right places, including his biceps.

Gabriel kept his brown hair cut to a medium length, and a light tan kissed his fair skin. But where his face had been bare before, he now had a well-groomed beard that gave him an urban cowboy look. He still wore a thin chain around his neck, the one Angeline had held onto countless times in moments of passion.

The way his jeans fit was both a blessing and a curse. Angeline's eyes lingered at his belt, tempted to dip lower. Once she realized she was caught, the little grin on Gabriel's soft lips giving it away, she broke eye contact and shifted her body away from him.

Holding his hat at his side, Gabriel anchored his other hand on his hip. A somber expression washed away his amused one.

"I've lost that privilege, calling you sweetheart. I know. But, it's a habit."

"Break it," she said, while attempting a quick exit from the hammock.

Gabriel offered his hand, but she ignored it.

"Angeline. Everything with us—" He paused, his face relaxing into an easy smile. "It's damn good to see you."

A bittersweet smile almost escaped her. She maintained control, keeping her expression blank. "Jury's still out on my end."

Gabriel had imagined this going so much better, but reminded himself, *At least she's talkin' to me, right?*

He put his hat back on. "About that sunrise, *this* view is better."

Always a flirt, Angeline thought as she continued up the pathway. If she turned around now, he'd see

189

the smile she was trying to hide. She kept moving until he called her name a second time.

A reply was ready on his tongue, but the moment Angeline turned and made eye contact, Gabriel froze. Instead of words, he grinned nervously, giddy as a damn schoolboy. He could say a million things right now, but most importantly, all the shit he *should* have said before.

As he considered the possibilities, he let his eyes roam, taking in every inch of her hourglass figure. Gabriel knew every curve, dip, and swell of her body. Angeline looked the same as the last time he saw her, save for the fact that her dark wavy hair was past her shoulders now.

Her brown skin was sun kissed and glowing, and when Gabriel stood by the hammock, the scent of her favorite conditioner, island coconut, drifted towards him. Once he got close enough, Gabriel knew he'd smell the cocoa butter of her lotion, too. It was an aroma that became an aphrodisiac, simply because it smelled so fucking good on her. He'd smelled it a thousand times when his skin had been pressed against hers.

As they stared at each other, Angeline wondered how one person could spark this many emotions within her. *Desire, joy, anger, longing.* Her mind spun, and her body yearned to be closer to his.

"Spit it out, Gabriel."

The words formed on his tongue, but he pushed them away and went with anger instead. "I *couldn't* give you a heads up. You blocked me on *everything.*"

"So, you *have* noticed." Deciding that this was all she could take right now, Angeline entered the house, slamming the door behind her.

Gabriel frowned, staring at the closed door and muttering to himself, "This might be the dumbest idea I've had in a long time."

* * *

An hour later, the mingled aroma of fresh coffee, pancakes, maple syrup, and homemade jam filled the room. The confusion of the morning had mostly settled down, for now.

The decision of whether or not to ask Gabriel to leave was left up to Angeline. Though her mind told her to slam the door in his face, she chose otherwise, suggesting they give him a test period of twenty-four hours. With that decision made, the day moved forward as planned.

The group of old friends reminisced about high school before the conversation shifted to adulthood and how life had been lately, all while trying to make the best of breakfast. Even as the occasional laugh, smile, or joke lightened the mood, Gabriel's presence created a layer of barely-contained tension.

Currently, Eva was telling a story that had the group engaged. Gabriel was half-listening as he glanced across the way at Daniel, who was watching him.

Everyone had their own feelings about the breakup, as well as about Gabriel showing up.

Daniel was torn; he and Gabriel had been best friends until the last two years had put some distance between them. Daniel was happy to see him, but worried about Angeline. Still, Daniel was rooting for them to get back together.

This was a sentiment others did not share, like Adele and Cyprien who thought they never should have dated in the first place.

"How's the tour?" Daniel asked.

"Starts next month," Gabriel answered while running his hand through his hair. A strand fell loose, touching his brows. Just as he started to smooth it back, his eyes met Angeline's.

"*Leave it, it looks good*," he heard in her voice, as clear as if she'd said it aloud.

His thoughts drifted to what he'd said earlier, about habits. Calling her *sweetheart* wasn't the only one. He kept things the way Angeline liked them; the cut and length of his hair, the style of belt he wore, his cologne. *If only I had—*

Gabriel stopped himself from heading down that road.

With a smirk, Cyprien asked, "Sure you want to hang with us regular folk?"

Cyprien had been the last to join their group. He was a transfer student at the time, and once he and Gabriel started a band together, the rest was history. Cyprien didn't believe Gabriel was ready for a committed relationship. Before Angeline, Gabriel had only had one serious relationship; everything else in between was just about having a good time. Cyprien didn't think Gabriel could offer the stability Angeline needed.

"Aren't you too famous for us now?" Adele chided.

As Angeline's best friend, she was one of the first people to know when Gabriel and Angeline had started fooling around. Adele always feared Gabriel was too much of a free-spirited charmer to be boyfriend material, and suspected he'd break Angeline's heart one day, which is exactly what happened.

Gabriel addressed the group. "C'mon, I hate when y'all say that. I just—I've been busy is all. I've got a lot to make up for. Let me start with this trip."

"You stopped coming to anything we planned, then—" Eva took a beat, eyes moving from Angeline to Gabriel, "... you two breaking up. It didn't feel right sending you an invite this year."

Eva was one of their biggest cheerleaders. She always wondered why Gabriel wasted his time with meaningless flings, and why Angeline dated men who looked good on paper, but were too conservative and boring for her. Even back in high school, though they dated other people, Eva sensed a spark between Gabriel and Angeline, and knew they'd one day be a couple.

Post breakup, Eva didn't pick a side. She tried to stay in touch with both of them, but when Gabriel distanced himself from everyone, he made it easy to just focus on Angeline.

"I would have chosen her, too," Gabriel replied, after a moment of silence.

He'd been a shit friend for the last two years, missed all the important milestones, stopped answering calls, and abandoned his old life as he lost himself in his new one. Amidst all that, he lost Angeline, too. Once that happened, Gabriel let himself drift even further away from the people he wanted to be around the most.

The person that Gabriel had spoken to most recently was Ricardo. Ricardo was the glue that initially got them all together in high school, combining two smaller friend groups into one. Their run in at the music venue was months ago. It had been a brief but joyful interaction, one that left Gabriel missing his friends... but not enough to pick up the phone and make things right.

Gabriel wasn't sure if all the friendships in the room were fixable, even if he turned up the charm. Adele hated him, but she was always Angeline's friend first. Daniel had been his best friend, so he might be able to get that back if he made the effort. Eva was a peacemaker at heart who just wanted everything to be normal again. But when it came to Cyprien, or Ricardo, Gabriel hadn't gotten a good read on them yet, leaving him reluctant to make the first move.

Ricardo spoke next, "I say we put him on chore duty."

Gabriel laughed. "You got a maid outfit for me too, I suppose?"

Daniel sat back, shaking his head. "How'd you find out about this anyway, man?"

"I have my ways," Gabriel grinned.

Adele pointed at him sternly. "Well, I'll tell you this—if you fuck up our trip, I'll kick your ass." She then dumped more sliced bananas on her pancakes, as if the matter was now closed.

Following her lead, almost everyone dove back into their plates, and side conversations resumed as Angeline poked absentmindedly at her pancakes.

"You okay?" asked Eva. She wished she could remove all the tension from the room and press the reset button. They'd had years of good memories in this vacation house, and at this very table, too. She missed how Angeline and Gabriel both shined when they were together, like they'd found their missing piece.

At the same time, Eva could vividly recall how Angeline cried in her arms after the breakup, and how depressed she'd been for months afterward. In contrast, instead of retreating into his shell, Gabriel denied his grief and regret, becoming a workaholic who couldn't stay in the same place for more than a few days.

"I'll be fine," Angeline shrugged, a mix of emotions thrashing inside of her. On one hand, crashing the trip was extremely selfish of Gabriel... but on the other, it felt kind of nice having him back.

Angeline offered Eva a half smile, then returned her attention to her breakfast.

* * *

Brilliant hues of red, orange, and pink streaked through the sky as the sun dipped below the horizon. As captivating as the spectacle was, all Angeline really saw was Gabriel.

Music filled the air as he strummed his guitar, his head lowered.

Some of the group had lingered inside, cooking and putting the finishing touches on dinner, while the rest gathered out by the lake.

The day had been a good one, filled with adventures, including seeing a spectacular waterfall during their hike. Soon, they'd eat dinner and follow that up with their game night tradition.

"I didn't plan on playin'," Gabriel said as he finished the tune.

"Why'd you bring the guitar then?" Daniel asked. "Come on, what you got for us?"

"I gotta sing for my supper now? Alright then, how about something new? This one's called, 'All of Me'." Gabriel glanced around the group, then began to play.

A lump lodged in Angeline's throat. She wasn't sure if she wanted to smile and move closer, or run and throw up. She tried to focus on anything but Gabriel's face, fixing her gaze on his guitar, but it did not help. She'd been with him when he bought it. He'd named it Aurora.

As Gabriel sang, Angeline's hard shell softened. The melodic music seemed to reach inside her, and she feared if she listened too closely, she might not find her way back. Focusing on the guitar again, her thoughts drifted to a memory.

* * *

"Go on, pick one."

"You should *not* leave that to me, you'll be the one playing it. It's your choice," Angeline replied, leaning against Gabriel's arm.

"We're not leaving here till you pick one. I trust your judgment."

"Really?" Angeline half-sighed, half-laughed, then crossed over to the guitars. "Fine. But don't get mad if you don't like how it sounds."

She took a look at the options, thrummed some strings, and finally settled on a beautiful mahogany acoustic model. "This is the one."

Hours later, they sat comfortably in her living room as Gabriel played a new song. Gabriel only glanced down as needed; the only thing he loved more than playing was seeing Angeline's reactions.

When the tune ended, Angeline smiled with her eyes closed. "That was lovely, Gabriel."

Setting the guitar aside, Gabriel moved closer to kiss her shoulder. "What can I say? You're my muse."

* * *

The sound of Gabriel's voice pulled Angeline back to the present. She found his eyes fixed on her, soulful as ever, full of regret and longing. She dropped her gaze from his face to his hands, her attention turning to the contours of his forearms and biceps, and how damn *good* he looked in his fitted shirt. But even directing her eyes to the ground didn't calm the heat rising within her.

Moments later, Angeline at last submitted to temptation and glanced his way, only to meet his steamy gaze head-on. Her heart fluttered.

Gabriel's eyes always told a story of a thousand words, even when none left his lips. It was simultaneously beautiful and sad, as communication had always been one of their issues.

Soon, her mind drifted once again to the past and one of the last fights they'd had before the breakup.

* * *

Angeline watched as Gabriel exited the stage. The crowd swarmed, praising his performance and asking to take photographs. He'd recently been featured as an up-and-coming artist, and his shows were growing larger by the day.

Usually, Angeline watched with a sense of pride and confidence; *That's my man up there.* But lately, she wasn't feeling so good about things. Jealousy and worry poked at her, especially when the female fans flirted so openly.

To his credit, Gabriel was good at stopping anything before it happened, and proudly let everyone know she was his girl... but Gabriel had always been a flirty guy, and sometimes her fears would get the best of her. Most shows, Angeline was able to push those feelings aside, but not tonight.

It was some minutes later when Gabriel made his way over to her. After a quick kiss, he led the way back to his dressing room.

"Why the frown?" Gabriel asked as he sank into a nearby chair. "It was a damn good night."

She sat on the edge of the table before him. "I've just been feeling a bit... insecure lately."

"You have nothing to worry about." He rose with a smile, cupping her face in his hands. "You know how I feel about you darlin'. I'm not going anywhere." He sealed the words with a kiss. "Hungry? There's this place—"

"No I don't want to eat, Gabriel, I want to talk!"

"There's nothin' to talk about! I'm with you, isn't that enough?"

"No, it's not."

"What... you want to sit in a circle and talk about my feelings? That's not really my thing. You're better at that anyway."

"Awareness isn't an excuse. Do better." With a heavy sigh, Angeline gathered her things and left the room, ignoring Gabriel's calls to her.

* * *

Feeling too close to the fire, Angeline quietly excused herself and headed to the house.

Soon midnight came, the early birds headed to bed, and the night owls busied themselves with other things. While Gabriel occupied himself with cleaning, Angeline headed to the lake alone.

At first, she simply wanted to sit by the lake and listen to the water. But when her thoughts became too loud, she opted for music instead. Slipping her earbuds in, she pressed *Play* on Gabriel's latest album. The broody guitar notes sounded first, followed by a melodic groove.

As the lyrics came in and Gabriel's voice seeped into her bones, she closed her eyes, the music sweeping her away to a land of *what-ifs* and alternate endings. Angeline had been telling herself for months that if he ever wanted to try again, she'd say no. Now... she wasn't so sure.

Angeline wanted to hate the music, to say that Gabriel didn't deserve his newfound success, but damn—he did, and something about this entire album felt *so* fucking personal. One song led to two, then three. It wasn't until she sensed someone approaching that she opened her eyes and turned the music off.

"Seeing as my maid duties are done, I figured I'd see what you were up to."

Angeline slid her phone into her pocket.

"What were you listening to, Buttercup?"

"Nothing you'd like."

He smiled as their eyes met. "You're as beautiful as ever."

Gabriel didn't look away, even when she did. For him, nothing compared to being under her hypnotic gaze, her almond-shaped eyes with their long lashes holding him in place.

Angeline fiddled with the strings of her hoodie, then gave in, giving him one quick glance. "Why are you here, Gabriel?"

He took the seat next to her. "For you."

Angeline pressed her lips together, tearing her eyes away from his.

Gabriel inched closer on the bench, then pulled a small notebook out of his back pocket. "Did you listen to the album yet?"

"No," she lied.

He nodded, then handed her the book. "Once you do—"

"I don't want this, Gabriel."

Gabriel took her hand, letting his touch linger before he placed the small notebook in her palm, then closed her fingers around it. "It's about you, Angeline. All of it."

Angeline nibbled her bottom lip while tightening her grip on the book. Tears welled up in the corners of her eyes, and almost without realizing it, she slipped it into her pocket.

Gabriel spoke softly as he dipped his head to be on her eye level. "I fucked up. I'm sorry."

Overwhelmed, Angeline rose to her feet and headed toward the house. Within seconds Gabriel was right behind her. He caught her left wrist with his hand, turning her to face him with one smooth motion.

He leaned in, taking a shallow breath before caressing her cheek with his thumb. Angeline's breath caught in her throat as Gabriel pressed his lips to hers.

Against her better judgment, she returned the kiss, settling one hand on the side of his neck and the other on his arm as she stood on her toes.

Gabriel's lips were soft against hers as their bodies pressed together. The floodgates opened; two years of longing, passion, and *what-ifs* came barreling through. Their quickened heartbeats drummed as one as Gabriel slid his fingers over the nape of her neck and into her hair.

Angeline moaned softly against his mouth, parting her lips, giving him permission to kiss her deeper. Without hesitation, Gabriel accepted, then embraced her and lifted her off her feet.

With her legs now wrapped around him, Gabriel held Angeline tight as the kiss grew in intensity. Her lips and tongue felt like silk against his own.

Her mouth tasted of chocolate and wine, and the heady scent of her amber perfume went straight to his cock.

In that moment, Gabriel felt more animal than man, a beast under the moonlight with one need— *her.* To taste her full breast with his lips, to bury his tongue between her thighs, to sink his cock deep inside her.

As the tantalizing visuals filled his mind, Gabriel grabbed at Angeline's ass with his free hand, still holding her tight with the other.

The ease with which Gabriel held her in his strong arms, the earthy scent of his skin, and the taste of aged whiskey on his tongue made Angeline's head spin. Memories of their past lovemaking flashed through her mind: the way her nails would trail over his back; his lips teasing and nibbling at that sensitive spot on her neck; the way he'd whisper, "*That's it, baby, just like that,*" as she rode him.

Angeline's back was against the house now, Gabriel pressing her into it as the kiss consumed them. Each pass of her nails in his hair, over the nape of his neck, and each time she dug her fingers into his shoulders sent Gabriel deeper into his feral state.

When the need for air could no longer be ignored, the kiss broke. Angeline nibbled at Gabriel's bottom lip before fully releasing it, their foreheads pressing together as they took deep, audible breaths.

Locking eyes with him, Angeline felt a storm within. There were so many ways this could go. She willed herself to be smart about this.

"Gabriel, we shouldn't." The words left her lips, and she knew it was the logical choice, but her body and heart didn't agree.

Gabriel stared at her with the softest eyes she'd ever seen, eyes full of everything that she hoped and wished he could have said before.

"I was a coward, Angeline. I was afraid of—"

"Don't." A spike of panic shot through her, and she pressed a finger to his lips. "*Don't.*"

He searched her eyes, "I need to say it."

"No," she shook her head, her mind fighting with her heart. "It's too late now, Gabriel."

His brows drew together as he gently let her down to her feet. Her knees weak, Angeline let the wall support her as she looked up at him.

"It's too late," she repeated, her voice breaking.

"What if it's not?"

The question tugged at her heartstrings, the desire to throw herself into his arms overwhelming. But she didn't let herself do that.

Instead, Angeline brushed her hand against his in silence. Disappointment filled his face, and Gabriel weaved his fingers through hers and let his head hang low. Angeline rested her forehead against his chest with closed eyes.

They stayed this way for a moment longer; Angeline savoring his scent, enjoying the feeling of holding his hand. She reveled in his touch; *home*. Gabriel was home.

But you worked so hard to move on. The thought cut through the warmth of their embrace like a knife. Pulling away, Angeline took her hand from his and then stepped aside.

"Goodnight, Gabriel."

When he didn't speak, she turned toward the door, resisting the urge to look back. Angeline entered the house, leaving Gabriel alone under the moonlight.

* * *

Angeline decided to work on her to-do list for the next day. It would be a welcome distraction from the kiss looping in her mind, and the taste of Gabriel on her lips. She was next in line to play chef, so busied herself gathering items and grouping them together in the fridge for tomorrow. Last on the list was wine.

After some time in the cellar, Angeline made her choices. Wines in hand, she made her way to the door but stopped short as she heard two familiar voices outside. She listened intently, recognizing

Gabriel's baritone.

"... we kept arguing... I was taking on more work and all she wanted to do was sit and talk our shit out, but the problems started before that. I couldn't even say the damn words, man. What the hell is wrong with me?"

"Wait. You never told her you loved her?" asked Daniel.

"No."

"Why?"

Gabriel sighed, "I dunno—"

"Cut the shit, man. You know."

"... because the last time I said 'I love you,' I got my heart smashed, okay? The girl before Angeline... I came there, heart in hands, all emotional and shit, saying the words and she not only didn't feel the same, she broke up with me the same fucking day."

"How come I didn't know about this?"

"Because I didn't tell anyone."

"You can't let one heartbreak ruin everything, Gabriel. Angeline is not her."

"I know... I fucking love her, D."

"Then act like it. You gonna whine about regrets, or are you gonna fix it?"

Angeline stepped back from the door, moving as quietly as possible. She abandoned the wines and slipped back to her room undetected.

With shallow breaths, she stared at her hoodie

in the center of the bed. Buried beneath that was Gabriel's journal, which she'd taken by accident. Over the next thirty minutes, she moved the journal multiple times, hiding it out of view, attempting to ignore it. But as the conversation she had overheard played in her mind, the desire to read the journal grew.

In those last months together, Angeline had wanted Gabriel to let her in, and now she finally had something to work with. A conversation overheard between friends and a small notebook would not hold all the answers, but she hoped that together they'd give her enough; enough to not feel foolish for falling for him in the first place, enough to convince her that what she knew in her heart was true, and not a fantasy.

Out by the lake, Angeline had done what she needed to do, not what she *wanted* to do. She'd wanted to stay there with Gabriel, fingers laced together and kissing under the moonlight as they entertained the idea of a second chance.

But it was smarter, wiser to just be done completely; and to be done, she had to believe that it was indeed too late—words that no matter how many times she said them out loud, left her inner belief shaky at best.

An hour later, Angeline sat on the bed, journal in hand, and it felt the weight of the world in her palms.

It seemed like a simple thing, a songwriter's note-book, but inside held a thousand emotions—truths said and unsaid, some of which she recognized as songs from his album, and lyrics to his newest tune.

Unsure of what she needed most; to scream, cry, dance in joy or set something on fire, Angeline was soon pacing as her thoughts spiraled. Minutes later, a knock came at her door. Six distinct raps. It was a pattern she knew well, one they invented together back in high school.

Gabriel spoke from the other side of the door, "I don't want to upset you. I just—you have my notebook." He forced a quiet chuckle, "Unless it ended up in the lake."

Before she'd fully decided what to do, Angeline was opening the door. Gabriel stepped over the threshold as she held the doorknob, looking up at him. Her grip tightened as she urgently searched his eyes for something: something she couldn't name, but desperately needed to know if it was there. Seconds later, she offered the small note-book, holding it between their bodies.

Gabriel bowed his head, "I can be shit with words sometimes—offstage at least."

"No shit," she commented.

"What I can't say, what I don't know how to say, I say it there, and with my guitar."

Angeline released the door handle, stepping back

inside the room. Taking that as an invite, Gabriel entered.

"And what were you trying to say?" She tossed the book at him carelessly, and he fumbled before catching it.

Gabriel sat on the bed with a heavy sigh. "You told me earlier you didn't want to hear it. You said it was too late."

"Try me."

Gabriel looked down at the notebook for a moment, flipping through it before putting it down on the bed. He looked up at Angeline with those deep blue eyes, and for the first time he laid himself bare. No guitar to use as a crutch, no veneer of charm to hide his heart.

Simple, vulnerable, *honest.*

"I screwed up. I pushed you away instead of opening up, and when shit got bad, I stayed on the road to avoid dealin' with it. You weren't overreacting. And... I miss you."

Angeline studied Gabriel while letting his words settle. It felt good to hear them; so good that it broke her somber expression. A dozen responses floated on her tongue, but before any of them could make it to her lips, she was moving toward him. Soon she was standing before him, Gabriel's eyes full of affection as he gazed up at her.

"Why couldn't you say that before? Why did you

wait until now?" The blunt questions were softened by her fingers tracing up and down his shoulder.

"Because I might be the world's biggest idiot. I lost you once before, but I won't make that mistake again."

Gabriel caressed the length of her arm, then loosely held her hand. A moment later, he drew her closer by her hips. He was completely under her spell, his body pulsing with desire and anticipation.

Angeline stood between his legs, playing with the chain around his neck as she closed the space between them. Logic gave way to pure need. As she kissed him, she wove her fingers through the soft waves of his hair once more.

Gabriel guided Angeline into his lap as the kissing intensified, their hands exploring each other's bodies; caressing and gripping, pulling and tearing at clothes with passion. His arousal ached, desperate to break free of the confines of his jeans so he could sink into her.

On the bed now, Angeline arched her back, creating friction between her aching core and his hard bulge, melting into Gabriel's touch as his hungry mouth tasted her bare breasts and hardened nipples. Each time his erection brushed against Angeline, a soft moan fell from her lips, making him even harder.

Gabriel's hunger for Angeline had plagued him

for so long he could no longer contain it. He slid inside her with ease, her warmth so inviting, the fit so *perfect* he nearly stopped breathing. He rested his head against her neck for a moment, letting himself savor every single sensation. Angeline ran her nails down his back as waves of pleasure consumed them both.

They soon found that sweet, passionate rhythm; like no time had passed at all. Angeline moaned, her eyes falling closed as she cupped his face with her hands, enjoying the weight of his body over hers. As she opened them again, she found Gabriel watching her.

He felt whole, for the first time in a long time. Suddenly, everything in the world made sense again. His pace slowed as he gazed deeper into her eyes, emotion welling up so quickly in his chest that he *had* to speak.

"I love you," he confessed, his heart so loud he could barely hear himself. "Always did. Always will."

Angeline's breath caught in her throat as she went still, her hands anchored on his back as her eyes widened.

Worry sparked in Gabriel during her silence, a string of '*oh fucks*' marching through his mind.

Slowly, her lips curved into a smile as her eyes lit up. "I love you too, Gabriel."

A sigh of relief fell from Gabriel as he cursed under his breath. "*Fuck*, baby. You scared me."

Angeline caressed his face as their confessions moved through her veins and rooted in her heart, right in the space she'd reserved for his words, the space that always had his name on it.

Moved beyond words, Angeline communicated her feelings with a kiss. A kiss that said everything it needed to and more, a kiss that inspired their hips to move again as he thrust inside of her and she gripped his ass to drive him in deeper.

Gabriel tried to keep his eyes open, to take in every single moan, every whimper. He wanted to see it all; the way her breasts bounced and how she'd grip at the sheets every so often—he was mesmerized.

Intoxicated by him, Angeline gripped his shoulders tight, locking her legs around his hips a little higher each time; a frenzied passion possessing them as they fucked harder and faster.

Gabriel was close to the brink now, losing his rhythm as Angeline's moans grew louder and louder. Every sound she made was music to his ears as the crescendo drew near.

Angeline passed the threshold first, sweet release rippling through her as his name fell from her lips. Her toes curled as she relaxed against the mattress, her legs still wrapped around him.

Gabriel sped up, fucking her through her orgasm

as he pinned her wrists above her head, thrusting until he could no more. He submitted to his release, resting his head against her soft breasts, time slowing as they basked in the afterglow.

Sometime later, as Gabriel dozed off and they lay wrapped in each other's arms, the bed sheets thrown across their legs, Angeline watched his face with adoration, tinged with worry. The thought echoed in her mind, *Will I regret this?*

Instead of dwelling on that, Angeline replayed Gabriel's confession.

"*I love you.*" Three words she had longed to hear the entire time they were together. Three words hidden in his songs, his caress, his kiss. Yet for some reason, Gabriel was so resistant to saying it aloud. A reason that was finally revealed and it wasn't due to anything Angeline had done wrong or was lacking; it was an old wound of Gabriel's that he needed to close.

But they were three words that Angeline had withheld, too, burying them deep inside to make herself less vulnerable. *Only if he says it first, then I can,* the promise she had made to herself a thousand times now ringing hollow and useless.

Gabriel stirred at her side, placing a kiss on her shoulder with half-closed eyes. "What's on your mind sweetheart?"

She returned the kiss, "Nothing."

His eyes closed again, as he caressed her arm. "Come to bed, turn your mind off a while."

Angeline smiled. Before, whenever she couldn't sleep, he'd say those very words. It was like a lullaby to her ears. Angeline cuddled against Gabriel, resting her head on his chest as he secured her in his arms, and minutes later she drifted off to the land of dreams. ♥

FALLEN STARS

♥ *by Maddie Swellkid*

She remembered the day they moved in, shortly before summer.

She was playing in her room with whichever neighborhood girl was paid to watch her that week, when her father called for her. She rushed down the stairs diligently, stopping abruptly in her tracks when she saw *him*.

A lanky boy. Not a kid anymore, not yet a teenager. Standing next to his mother in the entryway, he looked like he'd already seen too much, far too serious for his years.

She was younger, but she could tell.

Her own mother had been gone for less than two months, or so she thought. She couldn't be sure, time was still a tricky concept at her age. What she knew was that the house felt empty, and her days confusing without the rituals that used to punctuate them. There were no more bedtime stories. She ate most of her meals alone.

The boy told her his name, and offered his hand. His eyes were soft, his gaze familiar. He took her in as if he already knew her. As if he recognized her.

Following his example, she slid her tiny hand in his, saying her name. His palm was warm, his grip firm but gentle and hair rose on her nape, her skin tingling at his contact, as if her palm recognized his.

He held her grip, and she let him.

It took her a few days to notice her new mother's delicate beauty. How much the boy took after her. His lush, thick brown curls. His light amber skin and darker freckles. His deep mahogany eyes, tinted with something she couldn't name yet.

There were differences, too. His mother spoke in a strange accent. He didn't. Her face lit up when she looked at the girl's father. His didn't.

Her father had said, *Your new mother,* but not *Your new brother.* She remembered the tension, humming low between them. Something she sensed but never questioned. She herself called him *Father,* never *Dad* or *Daddy.* A man of very little affection and even fewer words, his presence in the house was scarce and icy.

Her new brother, however, was gentle. Quiet, at first.

Soon after they'd moved in, she slipped into his

room one evening, stealthy as a little ghost, thunder rolling down the hills in the distance.

He was lying on his bed, reading the thickest book she'd ever seen.

"I'm afraid of earthquakes," she told him in a little voice. She'd been sternly scolded before, for interrupting her father while he was reading the paper.

But the boy didn't send her back to her room. Instead, his eyebrows popped up over the top of the book, seemingly amused at her disarming earnestness.

"Okay. This is not an earthquake, though. Just a storm."

Through the window, lightning streaked the starless sky, highlighting angry clouds. Her eyes widened, flicking between him and the window pane. He set his book down, searching her face. His fingers were long, and his hands looked large; almost *too* large for his young body, as if some parts of him had grown faster than others.

"Do you know what to do, if there's an earthquake?" he asked her.

"No," she whispered, shaking her head.

She wanted to go sit next to him on the bed, but she was rooted into place, standing small on the threshold.

"You take cover under a desk, or a table," he said.

"And what if there's a volcano? I'm afraid of volcanoes, too."

His smile was soft. Understanding, and compassionate. He sat up straight, slinging his long legs over the side of the bed, and patted the mattress next to him, signaling her to come and sit.

"There's no volcano here. But there are, where I come from. Don't worry. I'll protect you. Okay?"

"Okay," she nodded, stepping in.

* * *

He was a guiding hand, splayed wide over her back, his heat radiating through her T-shirt as he taught her to ride a bike without the training wheels. He was a gentle stroke around her calf, blowing air over her scraped knees when she fell. A thumb brushing away hot tears from the roundness of her cheeks.

She reveled in the glimmer of pride that lit up his eyes at each of her successes. She learned there was another smile, beyond the friendly one he gave to strangers. A generous grin that dimpled his face, reserved just for her.

She learned his patience, his hands firm and steady underneath her belly as she splashed clumsily in the cool waves of the Pacific, his voice guiding her through the learning process.

He'd pack snacks and water, and they'd ride their

bikes side by side to the ocean. They'd spend the day at the beach, playing in the water until exertion weighed her sun-browned limbs and she went to sit on a towel, absent-mindedly brushing the sand off her legs, eyes trained on his dark silhouette swimming further and further.

She'd wake up to the sun kissing the horizon, his shirt draped over her small body. His sun-soaked skin next to hers exuded warmth, their shadows stretching long behind them.

From summer carnivals, to Halloween mazes, to winter wonderlands, they grew up together.

Often left on their own, they talked for hours on end, swapping the dreams and ideas hatching in their young minds. Languid afternoons bleeding well into the night, nestled in the sanctuary of his bedroom. Lying over the orange quilt his mother had made, she'd rest her face in the crook of his neck, while his long fingers tangled in her loose curls.

They traded books, her British classics, his science-fiction. Traded tapes, his 70s rock, her 80s pop. They watched movies together, and she learned the music of his husky laughter.

Soon, they could talk without words. Exchanging glances across the dinner table amid the growing distance between their parents; his fading mother, her selfish father.

Friends came and went, forever skating on the edge of their bond.

There were fights, sometimes, in the high school hallway. Boys mocking his name, or his skin, or his mother's accent. She learned his restraint, and the sudden flare of his temper. He'd come home with a bloodied lip and bruised knuckles.

Rage pulsated in her throat. She'd sit in silence behind him in the bathroom they shared as he cleaned his face. She plotted murder.

She watched him, intently, as his body changed. As he grew taller than anyone she knew. As his shoulders became so broad, he could fit her twice over in his strong embrace. As his voice dropped lower. As dark, coarse hair appeared below his navel, trailing a path down to the low waist of his swimming trunks.

She wondered if his searching eyes saw her in this new light, too. If he noticed the shaping curve of her waist, the blossoming swell of her breasts, the lengthening line of her neck.

When he went to parties, she tagged along, un-noticed by the older kids. Across a room full of drunk teenagers, his eyes would instantly find hers. She felt the caress of his mahogany gaze wrapped around her. Like a beacon, like a bright star in a dark sky, shining just for her.

When they walked together through crowds, his

large hand splayed over the small of her back, she felt invincible.

People wouldn't believe they were not blood siblings, arguing they looked identical. Two dark-haired, brown-eyed adolescents, alike in thinking and demeanor, one never seen without the other. But deep down, she knew none of what she felt was *normal*.

She'd watched enough sitcoms about stepfamilies starting over to see through the illusion. At school, her classmates complained about overbearing brothers trespassing on their privacy. Tales of constant bickering, rivalry, and irritation. She didn't understand any of those sentiments.

Instead, there was heat, simmering low and steady in her belly when he brushed her hair before bed. A racing in her chest when they sat together in the TV room and he rested his hand on her knee, his thumb drawing circles over her skin. That sticky thing, thick as honey, that dripped along her spine when she kissed her palm after he'd held her hand.

She knew she ought to feel shame. For all of this, and more.

For dreaming of licking the salt off his sun-warmed skin after a day at the beach. For sneaking into the bathroom at night and pulling his worn T-shirts from the laundry hamper, pretending the cottony fabric was his hands as she slipped them on over her bare body. For her coveting gaze over him, like a constant plea, and that hateful fire in her eyes whenever he talked to girls his age, with bigger breasts and plumper lips than she'd ever have.

And to some extent, she was ashamed. Or rather, she feared getting caught. She knew what *want* looked like. It was all over those other girls' pretty faces. How much of her own desire did *she* reveal?

Soon, she learned his focus and determination, when he started working around the neighborhood, fixing cars and mending furniture, saving every penny he earned to buy a truck. She was never far, sitting on a curb, on a stool, on a dirty garage floor—just about anywhere—as long as she could pretend to do her homework and watch him work.

With it, she learned the new sensation of his work-worn hands. Calloused palms, rougher fingers.

He found a beat-up red Jeep. Said it was a good bargain. Said, *This is for us.*

Eventually, he taught her how to drive.

They wandered further up north along the coast, and spent cool summer nights stargazing, lying side by side in the truck bed, his knuckles brushing against her thigh underneath the protective warmth of the orange quilt.

Content, she thought this would be her life forever.

But there were fights at home, too, and they got worse. They were not so engrossed in the world they'd built for themselves that they didn't notice what was happening to his mother. What her father was doing to her.

His mother kept getting worse, and he was quiet again. A crease formed in his brow, and she felt helpless.

During his senior year, he applied to several universities. With each admission letter he received, she vibrated with pride, thrilled by the prospect of his bright future. She was confused by his indifference, and questioned him relentlessly about it until he reluctantly explained that her father had refused to pay his tuition.

Outraged, she wanted to confront her father but he stopped her, pulling her into a full-body hug. A restraining embrace.

He tucked her face into the crook of his neck, cradled the crown of her head, stroked her hair. His skin absorbed her tears until her rage abated, until she felt nothing but the soothing rhythm of his steady heartbeat against the side of her face.

He told her this was for the best. That he'd already applied to the nearest community college so they wouldn't have to be apart. He told her he could save some money, and they'd go to college together.

After that, he worked twice as hard, and twice

as much. Dark circles shadowed his eyes. Exhaustion sharpened his features. He was barely home anymore.

Her days became endless, an ache felt in her bones, a longing for his presence. For his touch.

Wanting to help, she busied herself with babysitting, mowing lawns, tutoring middle-schoolers. He would not take her money at first, but eventually, he relented. Soon, however, she started finding gifts on her pillow when she came home at night. Books she'd borrowed more than once from the high school library. CDs to replace bootleg tapes. Stationery she had run out of.

She learned his observance, and relied on the eventuality of a restored balance. In the promise of their future.

In the end, none of it mattered. His mother died, and he left.

* * *

She remembered his last night, when he told her he was going away. She felt young, *too* young and scared, standing small on the threshold of his room again.

He was all shifting eyes, restless hands and pent-up tension, packing just a few belongings into a large black rucksack she'd never seen before.

She read the agony etched all over his expressive face, accentuating the crease in his brow, drawing his plush lips into a thin line, and she understood this was no ordinary goodbye. Instinctively, she sensed the threat of something definite. It seized her like a cold grip wrapped around her nape.

"Don't—*please*, don't leave me," she begged, trying to keep her voice level. She had to push the words out of her quivering chest, briskly wiping the stray tear she'd failed to blink away.

She learned the ticking of his jaw. The gritting of his teeth. She learned what *cold* truly meant, when his gaze wouldn't meet hers.

He paused, and his eyes glimmered in the semi-darkness, their mahogany depth highlighted by unshed tears.

"I can't stay," he answered, his voice unsettlingly quiet. He seemed to hesitate before he added, "Sooner or later, he's gonna kick me out. I won't give him the satisfaction."

"Then take me with you!" she pleaded with renewed hope. "I'll work. I can support both of us."

He closed his eyes, and she knew the telltale sign of his resolve. Her heart sank.

"I can't. I've enlisted."

His answer cut through her tender flesh, the irreversible consequences of his decision worse than *anything* she could have imagined.

"You did *what*?" she asked in a shrill voice.

"Joined the pilot training program," he said, facing away.

Hunched over his bag, he hid his face from her, and the extent of his betrayal shook her like an earthquake. Her fear became incomprehension, incomprehension became anger. It spread through her like a wildfire, painting her vision red, crumbling her inner world into a wasteland of ashes.

"If you go through with this, you will never see me again," she threatened.

He heard her, and yet, he was gone in the morning.

She was alone with her father again.

* * *

After a handful of years, she also left, flying across the country to build a life for herself. A life all her own.

In the hollowness of this new life, she learned to name what had colored his eyes. What came and went like a high tide throughout their years together.

Melancholy.

The word sat on her tongue, heavy, bittersweet. She could taste it on her palate. Most days, she couldn't find the strength to talk around it.

His absence couldn't be learned. Nor could she get used to the worry that ripped through her chest in her dreams, clinging to her skin long after she'd woken. In those dreary mornings, she'd lift her eyes to the sky, addressing a silent prayer. *Let him be safe.*

She hardened, sustained by resentment, isolated by loss. She let hope die, and years turned into a decade.

Until she came home one Friday to find him sitting on the flight of stairs leading up to her apartment building's doorstep, the black rucksack at his feet.

The shock knocked the air from her lungs. Blood rushed to her feet, dark circles clouding her vision, and for a few terrifying seconds, she thought she would faint.

There he was, before her. Safe and sound, as much as she could tell. Relief washed over her, more powerful than anything she had ever experienced. A lump formed in her throat. It prickled the corner of her eyes, obliterating everything else, thawing away the very resentment that had kept her upright until then.

He stood up, propping his hands on his hips, and she took in his massive silhouette. She had to back away a few steps. A patchy beard shadowed his cheeks. Wrinkles had formed around his eyes. His curls were flattened under a trucker hat, the strands poking out around his ears were darker. The crease in his brow that she remembered so well had become permanent.

Her mind was unable to comprehend those changes, his presence even less. But her body recognized him. Her body would know him in death.

Disoriented, lightheaded, she briefly wondered how much she'd changed in his eyes. The size of him, the years on him, rekindled the want that her grief had smothered.

He spoke first.

"I need a place to stay for a few days," he said, without any other preamble. His voice was gruff, hoarse, as if he hadn't used it for years.

"What are you, on leave or something?" she asked. The aggressiveness in her tone surprised her. His eyes wouldn't meet hers, his face remained concealed in the shadow of his hat brim, and it made her furious.

"No," he slowly shook his head. "I'm done. Got a discharge."

He paused, and her mind reeled with the implications. Bewildered, she wondered if her desperate threat had kept him away from her all these years.

He shifted on his feet, folding his strong arms

over his chest. "I just need a couple days to sort things out. I'll find something else if—"

"No! No, you can stay here."

She didn't ask how he'd found her. Instead, she let him in, and the following day, she bought sheets for the couch.

A week went by in hostile silence.

When she woke up in the morning, he was already out. He'd always been an early riser. When she came home from work in the evening, he hardly acknowledged her. Without asking her, he repainted her apartment. Fixed whatever needed to be fixed. It only fueled her confusion and fanned her smoldering anger. She spoke not a word. Deep down, she was thankful for the strong smell of paint that covered his scent.

She felt stuck. Stuck in her small apartment, with his body too close, new yet familiar. Stuck in her head with a million questions about the things he had seen and the ones he had done. About the dimness in his eyes, about the shadows on his face. About the scars on his skin and the tiny tattoo on his hand. About what had *really* driven him away, and what had brought him back after so many years.

Her days were haunted by the memories of their drives along the coast and the starry nights in the truck bed that left her muscles sore and her heart content. Of their bike rides to the beach, sand turning up everywhere for days afterward, in her bed, her school bag, her hair.

Despite herself, she longed for those languid sunny afternoons tucked away in his embrace. She yearned for the days when she knew his heart better than her own. When her world was contained in his touch, and her safety in the curve of his neck.

At night, she lay awake in bed, tucked under the old orange quilt, ears trained on the sound of his breathing in the room next to hers. In the blue morning hours, silent tears streaked her face, one for each piece of him she'd unlearned over the years. Once, his voice had been her favorite music. Now, his silence was a deafening partition between them. His shifty gaze an unfathomable ocean.

Every day, she'd come home with the resolve to talk to him. Every day, his avoidance defeated her. It felt like drowning.

The following Friday, she asked one of her coworkers out, a younger man. A couple of drinks was all it took for him to follow her to her place. She wasn't sure of what she was trying to achieve, she only knew she was desperate, and she needed a detonator.

When they stepped into her living room, she saw her brother's frame tense, thick muscles bunching under his threadbare t-shirt.

A perverted relief slackened her chest. There was

life in his eyes, at last, when he glowered at her.

Halfway through an awkward introduction, he interrupted her with a grunt.

"Get him out of here."

Her coworker huffed uncomfortably. "I'm sorry, who are you again?"

"I'm her brother," he growled, staring straight at her.

"You have a brother?"

"He's not my brother," she said.

"I *am* your brother, and you get him out of here now, or I *fucking* will," he snarled, teeth bared.

The air stood still around them, thick and heavy and ready to burst. With an empty apology, she ushered the young man out. As soon as the door closed, she turned around to see him facing away from her again, grabbing his black rucksack from the floor.

"Coming here was a fucked-up idea," she heard him say over the din of her pounding heart. "I gotta leave. Haven't done all this for nothing."

"Why did you come, then?" she asked, her voice shaking with apprehension, with repressed fear, with built-up resentment.

"I shouldn't have," he snapped back, shoving a shirt into the bag.

She balled her fists, blinking back the tears that weighed down her eyelids and undermined her strength. Shaking her head, she readied herself to hold him back, forcibly if necessary, when a thought crossed her mind.

I'm not asking the right question.

A fleeting hunch, but she caught its tail and held on tight.

She drew in a deep breath, and his name blossomed inside her chest.

Painful, at first. Sprouting from under the heavy stone she'd forced over it for the past fifteen years. From the tip of her lips, to the curl of her tongue, to the back of her throat, the syllables echoed between them.

He froze. Seconds dragged empty, like her years without him.

Slowly unfurling to his full height, he turned to face her. Her gaze traced the tension in his weary features. She steeled herself.

"Why did you leave?" she asked.

He winced, flexing his jaw, and she knew she'd hit the mark.

"Was it really because of my father?" she pressed, taking a first step in his direction.

He persisted in his silence, but she kept moving closer, and with each step, she grasped at something familiar. Minute expressions she could read. Wordless emotions that only she could decipher. That tendon she'd seen ticking in his jaw every time he faced her father and tried to hold back his temper. His chin held high, his cold hard stare, a warning to the boys provoking him in the high school hallway.

She knew him then, she knew him still, and she hung on to that certitude with renewed faith. Tonight, she wouldn't let him push her away.

Standing before him, she tipped her head up. Her eyes bored into his, spearing through their defiance, through their infinite sadness.

Imperceptibly, he lowered his face. His eyebrows shifted, the slightest drop, softening his gaze.

Melancholy, she thought, and she tasted the word, standing so close to his heaving chest that her skin thrummed with his heartbeat.

Melancholy, tinting his eyes when his gaze found hers across a room of drunk teenagers, across a hallway of boisterous highschoolers, across an ocean of faces.

Melancholy, a look so familiar, and yet she'd only been able to name it after he'd left.

But he was here now, standing in front of her, and tonight, she realized it might be something else, something more. She recognized in him what she'd been hiding for years. A plea. A longing. A secret.

Her eyes widened, and she faltered under his stare, comprehension slowly blooming inside her brain, trickling down her back and raising chills in its wake.

His throat worked with a hard swallow, as if he'd been dreading that realization for years. As if, perhaps, he'd been waiting for it.

"I left to protect you," he surrendered.

"Protect me from what?" she murmured, breathless.

"Protect you from me. From the things I..." he trailed off, his voice a sinking husk.

Images flashed through her mind like still frames, his outstretched hand, his dimpled smile, his bloodied lip. The outline of his silhouette, swimming further and further.

"From the things I wanted. Want still," he finished, his tone firmer.

She splayed her hands over his solid chest, for balance, for anchoring. She felt the beating of his heart under her palms, stronger than she remembered. The body of a grown man.

He tried leaning away from her but she sought the contact of his skin. Rising to her tiptoes, she nuzzled the sharp edge of his jaw, feeling the pricking of his beard. She inhaled him there, filled her lungs with his heady scent, and the firm muscles of his chest trembled underneath her palms.

"I am your *brother*," he gritted.

She shook her head, cheek brushing against his skin.

"You're my *everything.*"

He let out a pained growl, gripping at her waist with a push, but she burrowed into him, into his neck, into his scent.

"I walked beside you in dreams," she said.

"You walked beside me everywhere," he answered in an exhalation.

His hand traveled her body to her nape, fingers carding through her hair, angling her head up. His gaze fell to her lips. With a quiet gasp, she parted them.

"I wanted this," he whispered, his voice a raspy murmur. "You. All of you. To myself."

His words dripped along her spine like honey, thick and golden. She felt liquid fire in her bloodstream, a tidal wave coursing through her veins.

Their lips met—a perfect fit, a full circle, a foregone conclusion. He kissed her full and deep, strong arms circling her waist, lifting her from the floor. Crushing her against him, as if to meld their two bodies into one.

Urgency bled into their embrace, large hands roaming her body, more bites than kisses as he scraped his teeth along the line of her throat. She moaned into his violence, she wanted so much more.

Take me, she thought, *eat me whole, make me yours.*

"I will," he growled.

Later, she would learn his devotion and reverence. When, spent and sated, he'd lay her over the orange quilt, moving over her, trailing her skin in sharp kisses paired with gentle touches. Inch by inch, un-hurried and methodical. Calloused palms, rougher fingers.

But first, she learned his intensity. Learned the weight of him around her and inside of her. The tender ache of his insatiable hunger for her.

She learned his taste, and he drank hers.

He said, *My love for you is like a knife through my chest. My heart beats around it.*

He held her in his arms, pressed against his chest, his hold strong and unyielding.

"Say my name," he said, as he came deep inside her.

She did, releasing the weight of her unspoken longings, of her wistful want and her unyielding love, years and moments held close between her lips, shaded and hidden.

They fell upward to the stars. ♥

IDLE HANDS

♥ *by J.L. Valdés*

Lourdes had always been obsessed with hands. Men's hands, to be exact. It was the first thing she always noticed. Couldn't help herself, really. During adolescence, when crushes blossomed quick as tulips in the spring, fingernails chewed down to nubs could squash them with just as much speed.

They weren't the only thing she cared about. Lively eyes of any shade could entrance her, a charming smile, a sense of humor, of course—these were all essential—but it was the *hands* that usually either broke, or sealed the deal.

Rafael had the *loveliest* hands. Long fingers, clean and neatly trimmed nails, fingertips and palms callused from hard work. She thought about them as she padded throughout their dimly lit kitchen, the way they'd pulled her closer in the dark cave of their bedroom. She smiled to herself, still feeling the ghost of his touch on the small of her back while she brewed the first pot of coffee of the day.

Lourdes managed to get the pot in place just as she heard his footfalls overhead. Regret swirled in her gut for a moment that she had forgone time which she could have spent tangled up with him in their bed, but it was replaced with the anticipation of him finding her waiting for him in the kitchen, coffee steaming.

The coffee machine did its thing, and the comforting smell of the first few drops pulled at the corners of her mouth. She couldn't help but reminisce about how they'd met.

At a coffee shop. So cliche, the memory still made her eyes roll halfway back into her skull. He'd walked in—no, *strode* in.

Rafael then, just as he does most of the time, exuded confidence. Not in an overtly cocky, obnoxious way, but in the way that men who don't question their place in this world often do. He'd smiled at her, then looked her up and down with those dark eyes like he was getting ready to eat her alive.

Lourdes would have let him, too, if he'd approached her that way—but he hadn't, he'd been a perfect gentleman.

She'd noticed his hands right away; the way they curled around his coffee cup, those long, thick fingers with perfectly manicured nails. He'd had her eating right out of them, and Lourdes never looked back.

The coffee maker sang its mechanical song to signal a job well done, and Lourdes made her way over to pour the steaming elixir into Rafael's favorite mug, just as he made his way down the stairs.

"You are an *angel*." He smiled the smile he saved only for her, and she beamed back at him, heart pounding at his presence, despite all their time together.

"I do my best." She watched as his hands engulfed the mug she still clutched and warmth followed, both from the mug and his palms.

"You spoil me, is what you do." He groaned and she almost felt it somewhere in his chest, the sound filled her head with visions of the previous night, when he'd made the same sounds in a very different context. His smile widened and she knew he could see the blush blooming in her cheeks.

"I'll be home early tonight, wear something nice." Rafael's tone was light, but her heart raced all the same.

"Are we going somewhere fancy?" Her long, delicate fingers threaded through his almost too-long hair, fixing where he'd tucked it behind his ear.

He'll need a cut soon, Lourdes thought to herself, but at that moment it was perfect—pitch black, thick and smooth, as opposed to her soft brown waves. Perfectly at odds with his immaculately tailored suit.

"I doubt we'll see any royalty, just a nice dinner. Thank you for the coffee, my love." He pulled her close, hand sweeping down to splay at her lower back and his mouth pressed against hers in a soft kiss.

"I'll see you soon." He pressed his lips to the side of her neck, his soft breath summoning goosebumps across her body. With a quick crack of that big palm on her ass, he pulled away and made his way out the door.

Lourdes squealed at the impact, smiling at his back until she was alone.

Her desire for him lingered throughout the day, a low simmer on the back burner of everything she did. She would indulge for a moment, taking a break from her work to ponder exactly where it was he would be taking her, what exactly he had planned and her mind filled with visions of them dancing. Or being whisked away to some private menu tasting by a highly decorated chef she'd never even heard of.

Those things would be wonderful, and she loved everything Rafael planned, mostly because he'd taken the time to *plan* it. But what she really wanted was him. Just him.

She bit her lip, typing away at her computer while

practically feeling his mouth on her neck, on her breasts, between her legs. She thought about how he loved to tease her, to get her so worked up she begged for him to just hurry up and *fuck* her already. She let out a sigh, both impressed and annoyed that he managed to send her into a frenzy, just by the power of her own recollection.

When it came time to start getting ready, Lourdes took leisure in it, going slowly as if performing a ritual.

She lingered in the shower, teasing herself with the same thoughts that had plagued her since that morning. Her fingers danced along her skin, over her thighs, plucking at her nipples, swirling over her clit long enough to make herself ache, but ultimately denying herself any sort of release.

Lourdes brushed and styled her hair, long and shiny, then perfumed herself with the scent that she knew made Rafael skim his nose across her shoulders with a growl. The dress she settled on was on the longer side, but the cut of it accentuated her quite nicely. She found it tasteful, yet suggestive.

He came home early, catching her as she put on her earrings.

"You look beautiful." Rafael leaned against the door frame, watching her with a playful leer painted on his face, his eyes tracking her as she flitted about the bedroom, adding her finishing touches.

"Thanks, baby, I just need to grab my purse and I'm good to go." She met his eyes, and she was pleased to see that his expression mirrored hers. She saw the same want, the same self-imposed torture in them.

"One more thing." He moved towards her, and not for the first time did she feel that dropping feeling in her belly, the sudden fall on a roller-coaster, the butterflies swarming.

"What is it?" Her cheeks lit up as he got closer, towering over her despite the heels she had on.

Rafael said nothing as he kneeled at her feet and brought his hands to her ankles. He swept them up her calves, lifting the bottom of her dress as he slid them up her thighs until he curled his fingers under the band of her panties, and slipped them down her legs.

Lourdes watched him with bated breath, bare and trembling as he pressed his lips to the dark patch of hair at the junction of her thighs before grasping and lifting one foot, then the other to remove her underwear completely. She felt delicate, his large hands wrapped around her ankle, long fingers nearly touching.

"These are mine now," said Rafael. He stood, holding the tiny scrap of silk as she watched him, mesmerized and aching more than ever before. Her lips parted, her eyes glazed as he pressed them to his nose, breathing the scent of her in for a moment. Then he smiled, and folded them into the pocket of his suit jacket.

"After you." He held out his hand, the gears in Lourdes's mind that had paused finally whirred up and began to turn. She took his hand and they left for the night.

She couldn't keep her eyes off his hands, and he knew it. He flexed them when he turned the steering wheel, the white knuckle grip sending her into a frenzy. He smiled to himself, catching Lourdes with her lip trapped between her teeth. When he took one off the wheel to land heavy on her thigh she sighed, and covered it with her own.

The size of his hands always made her brain buzz. They were huge and warm, dwarfing her smaller ones. She traced the lines of them, following a prominent vein, and envisioned herself following it with her tongue as she had countless times before.

She remembered the feeling of it wrapped around her delicate neck, holding her still while he drilled into her. She felt them at her breasts, on the meat of her ass, holding her thighs open for his tongue.

"What are you thinking about?" His voice was playful, but knowing, and for a moment she felt caught.

"Lots of things."

"Dirty things, I bet. You got that faraway look in

your eye, and if I didn't know you any better I'd be jealous." He laughed.

"Hmm... well, maybe you should be." Lourdes lifted his hand from her thigh, threading her fingers with his. She pressed her lips to the back of it, a mirror of what he usually did to her. "Maybe I'm imagining someone giving me the night of my life."

"Are you, now? Maybe I ought to put you over my knee, spank you for being such a bad girl."

Her heart raced and she could see it, *feel* it. His heavy palm, the resounding crack, the sting and then the soothing caress. The splotchy, fiery red marks she'd proudly wear. Warmth bloomed on her face and in her belly.

"*Although*—you might enjoy it a little too much." His eyes found hers at the red light, caught again.

The restaurant was dimly lit, creating an intimate atmosphere despite every table being occupied.

"When did you make these reservations?" Her eyes scanned through the tastefully modern dining room; it looked and felt exclusive.

"Never mind that." Rafael smiled, enigmatic, but she saw through it. This had to have been booked well in advance, it was too packed for him to have snagged a table at the last minute.

He ordered good wine, a whole bottle. Dark red and strong, and it paired beautifully with the food, but it was all secondary to the undercurrent of the lust Lourdes had suffered the whole day. The conversation and laughter flowed easy, the two of them sequestered in their own comfortable familiarity, hours passing as they talked about anything and everything. It all inevitably led back to the craving though. The intense *want* they had for each other.

His eyes devoured her, undressing her boldly with just a sweep over her form. Her cheeks flushed a pretty pink when his tongue came out to trap his bottom lip and pull it into his mouth, and again when he reached into his jacket and pulled out the balled up wad of her panties and pretended to use them as a napkin.

"*Raf, put those away!*" Her voice was a nervous whisper, but he only laughed low, and leaned closer to press a kiss to her throat.

"I can smell you on them, it's making me crazy." He pressed another kiss to her cheek, looking for all the world like a gentleman to the unassuming eye.

Lourdes took a deep breath, attempting to steady herself but he was relentless. He swirled his finger around the rim of the wine glass, slow. She could almost feel it, the soft swirl of his finger at her clit.

It was too much, and she had half a mind to excuse herself to splash some cold water on her face. Before she could do anything, though, he was signaling to the waiter, asking for the check.

The drive home was another form of torture. Rafael seemed to luxuriate in driving her mad with his hand, big and strong and pulling her dress up to land heavy on her skin. He took the long way home, all while drawing little patterns high on her inner thigh, close to where she was bare and soaked for him.

The arousal was choking her, wrapping around her throat, around her thighs, snaking its way through her insides to make her melt into the heated leather seats of his car.

Her mind kept replaying a perverted montage of them, tossing around on their bed. Visions of him holding her open for his gaze, for his tongue, for his fingers, for his cock swam through her lust-addled imagination. So much that it kept her quiet, her eyes closed and her lip caught between her teeth.

The car stopped and when Lourdes opened her eyes they were home, the engine off with him staring at her, his expression mirroring every dirty thought she had. They smiled at each other, knowing, the silence pregnant with the promise of things to come.

Silently, he got out and opened her car door, offering his hand to help her out, then sliding it around to rest on the swell of her ass as he opened the door.

"After you," Rafael gestured at the open door.

Lourdes walked inside, her stomach a mess of nerves and arousal as she headed directly for their bedroom. Her face lit up with a smile at the feel of him following closely behind her, both of his huge, warm palms coming to rest on her hips as she climbed the stairs. ♥

ABOUT THE AUTHORS

Editor **Anisa Larkwood** (she/her) lives in Austin, Texas. Most weekends you can find her drinking a huge mug of coffee and writing, or snuggling with her black cat while reading. Anisa published her debut novella *Surrender* in 2023, and she's now hopelessly addicted to writing and releasing *"spicy"* books. She blames Jasmine Luck for sparking her self-publishing dreams in the first place. See more at AnisaLarkwood.com

Editor/Contributor **Jasmine Luck** (she/her) is an Anglo-Asian writer living in the UK. Her short stories have appeared in the multicultural anthology *Love All Year*; the anthology *Have Ship, Will Travel*; and the *Home for the Holidays* collection by Stories Rule Press. In 2015 she won a CTRR award for a paranormal novella (writing as Jasmine Aherne). She lives with her patient husband and one son, and likes cats a normal amount (and you can't prove otherwise). See more at Instagram.com/jazzyluckwrites

Contributor **O.J. Adira** (she/her) is a Minneapolis-based theater artist with a BA in English Literature from the University of Minnesota Duluth. While she uses it mostly to construct industry grants and award-winning scripts, she treats herself by reading and writing romances in her down time. Nothing makes her happier than the combination of world travel, a nice desert, a pretty sunset, and a Kindle full of juicy fanfiction.

Contributor **Charlie Gallows** (she/they) lives in Minnesota with her husband and their three children. She spends her free time writing fiction, daydreaming, and laughing. See more at Linktr.ee/charliegallows

Contributor **Jayce Hanna** (they/them) has an appreciation for all things 80s, and a good hug makes them weak in the knees. They share their apartment with cat-like creatures hellbent on making sure no one in the household gets enough sleep, and that no story gets written without at least one <*sefkjNÅWR9*. See more at Instagram.com/jayce.hanna

Contributor **Viola Layne** (she/her) has dreamt of being a writer since she was a child. A voracious reader who devours books, she's constantly crafting stories on paper when available, and in her head when it isn't. She's excited to share her first published story with you in this anthology. See more at Instagram.com/violalaynewrites

Contributor **Olivia Lockhart** (she/her, "Livvie" to her friends) is an English author who can't quite decide if she wants to write contemporary romance or paranormal romance. Either way, it HAS to be romance! She loves to write about the underdog, the one who got away, the bits of love stories that we can all relate to. Livvie has published three books so far, and regularly writes steamy shorts for Medium. When not writing she can be found drinking wine, cuddling her beloved pooch, or with her head buried in a book. See more at Instagram.com/livvieharts

Contributor **Sabine Marlize** (she/her) has always wanted to do it all, and is happy that she can now say she's a published writer, too. Quarantine made her start pouring her daydreams into stories and screenplays in her late 20s. When she's not writing, watching movies, or petting bunnies... she's probably curating her Pinterest, trying out new recipes, planning her next trip, or petting cats. This is her first published work under this pen name.

Contributor **Cate Page** (she/her) is a wife, mom, and teacher from the Triangle Area in North Carolina. She's been writing since middle school and has been obsessed with superheroes for just as long. She loves reading a wide variety of books including romance, historical fiction, comedy, biographies, and comic books and manga. She's also a big, big, *big* Star Wars fan. When she isn't spending time with her daughter and husband, she is usually found listening to music, exercising, or building Lego sets. See more at Instagram.com/catepagewrites and TikTok.com/@catepagewrites

Contributor **Quinn Perry** (she/her) is a 27-year-old writer hailing from the Midwest, carrying a bit of southern soul in her storytelling. She's been putting pen to paper since her early teens, crafting poetry and narratives that celebrate the complexity of Black women. When she's not writing, you can find Quinn gaming with her friends, tracking down the best new coffee spots, or deep-diving into her ever-expanding playlist. Quinn is committed to creating stories that center Black women in all their vibrant, authentic glory—because she believes they deserve to see themselves in every kind of story. See more at Instagram.com/quinnethperry

Contributor **Carmilla Sloane** (she/her) resides on the East Coast, though her heart is always in New Orleans. Often writing or reading, books on astrology, divination, and herbalism are amongst her prized collection. When she's not in the city, Carmilla explores magical places in her best goth attire. See more at Instagram.com/carmillasloane

Contributor **Maddie Swellkid** (she/her) is a French archivist and lifelong Star Wars enthusiast who lives in Paris. When she's not writing about soulmates and forbidden love stories, or day- dreaming about being a vampire and the Roaring Twenties, she's most likely to be found visiting a museum or going to the movies. Harboring a lifelong fascination for time-travel, her Roman Empire is... the Roman Empire.

Contributor **J.L. Valdés** (she/her) hails from the wilds of Canada, and enjoys cuddling up with a ludicrously large iced coffee and a good horror novel. She has been telling stories ever since she could string two sentences together, and writing them since she could hold a pencil. Her true passion is writing romance and thrillers. She is currently working on her first novel, and wanders the aisles of her local bookstore when she needs a break. This is her first publication.

ALSO BY
ANISA LARKWOOD
& JASMINE LUCK

Look for these titles wherever you buy your books!

Surrender
by Anisa Larkwood

Tara French is accustomed to chaos. She's been in and out of trouble her whole life, danced in strip clubs for years, and now she's on the run with $800,000 stolen from her mobster ex-boyfriend. Tara is lonely after months of hiding out, so when she sees the opportunity for a tryst with a handsome stranger at a bar, it's too tempting to resist.

David Price is always in control. His work as an intelligence agent, his moonlighting as a hired assassin, and his bland cover life in suburbia are planned down to the smallest detail. But when he hooks up with Tara, she pushes a button he normally keeps hidden, and Dave's submissive side comes out.

Tara and Dave part ways thinking they'll never see each other again... but a sudden attack on Tara outside the bar thrusts Dave into saving her life. Dave assures Tara that he can get her out of danger, but Tara suspects that Dave isn't telling her the whole truth about himself. When confronting him directly doesn't work, she ties him up and teases him to break through his defenses.

Can Dave fully surrender to Tara, or will his need to stay in control put her life in danger?

Sugar Rush
by Jasmine Luck

An escape across the Atlantic, where she can cover her cousin's bakery and test out her popular Asian-fusion treats, is the healing distraction Londoner Maddie Liu needs after her failed engagement.

Her bags are only packed for a few weeks, but the family friend who collects her at the airport is an unexpected and irresistible temptation.

Rick Callahan left the Army to take over his dad's carpentry business and make a home for his sister and her son. He keeps himself busy providing for them, so there isn't time for romance in his mind. But everything changes when he meets Maddie, and they realize how much they need each other.

Family and friends help Maddie feel at home, but it's Rick who makes her yearn to stay, even though the career she has built is across an ocean.

When her past shows up in Kentucky, and the date of her return flight creeps closer, Rick and Maddie must decide if their sugar rush is worth the risk.

Jasmine Luck is also the author of novels *Say You'll Stay, One Minute to Midnight,* and *Purrsuasion.*

Printed in Great Britain
by Amazon